W9-ARX-791

If only Nate hadn't fallen asleep in the sun, giving her the opportunity to admire him.

But when Claire realized what she was doing, where her thoughts were leading, she quickly jerked her gaze away.

All Claire knew about romance, sex and men, she'd gotten from books. All she knew about happy marriages she'd learned from reading about them. A dream of having love in her life was just that. A dream. She had to be ever-vigilant to keep that kind of dream from surfacing; from allowing it to take over her life and permitting her to become dissatisfied with her lonely existence.

Her dream must remain her secret; her secret wish....

Dear Reader,

Silhouette's 20ᵗʰ anniversary celebration continues this month in Romance, with more not-to-be-missed novels that take you on the romantic journey from courtship to commitment.

First we revisit STORKVILLE, USA, where a jaded Native American rancher seems interested in *His Expectant Neighbor*. Don't miss this second book in the series by Susan Meier! Next, *New York Times* bestselling author Kasey Michaels returns to the lineup, launching her new miniseries, THE CHANDLERS REQUEST.... One bride, *two* grooms—who will end up *Marrying Maddy*? In *Daddy in Dress Blues* by Cathie Linz, a Marine embarks on his most terrifying mission—fatherhood!—with the help of a pretty preschool teacher.

Then Valerie Parv whisks us to a faraway kingdom as THE CARRAMER CROWN continues. *The Princess's Proposal* puts the lovely Adrienne and her American nemesis on a collision course with...love. The ever-delightful Terry Essig tells the tale of a bachelor, his orphaned brood and the woman who sparks *A Gleam in His Eye*. Shhh.... We can't give anything away, but you *must* learn *The Librarian's Secret Wish*. Carol Grace knows...and she's anxious to tell you!

Next month, look for another installment of STORKVILLE, USA, and THE CHANDLERS REQUEST...from *New York Times* bestselling author Kasey Michaels. Plus, Donna Clayton launches her newest miniseries, SINGLE DOCTOR DADS!

Happy Reading!

Mary-Theresa Hussey

Mary-Theresa Hussey
Senior Editor

Please address questions and book requests to:
Silhouette Reader Service
U.S.: 3010 Walden Ave., P.O. Box 1325, Buffalo, NY 14269
Canadian: P.O. Box 609, Fort Erie, Ont. L2A 5X3

The Librarian's Secret Wish

CAROL GRACE

Silhouette
ROMANCE™
Published by Silhouette Books
America's Publisher of Contemporary Romance

If you purchased this book without a cover you should be aware that this book is stolen property. It was reported as "unsold and destroyed" to the publisher, and neither the author nor the publisher has received any payment for this "stripped book."

 SILHOUETTE BOOKS

ISBN 0-373-19473-0

THE LIBRARIAN'S SECRET WISH

Copyright © 2000 by Carol Culver

All rights reserved. Except for use in any review, the reproduction or utilization of this work in whole or in part in any form by any electronic, mechanical or other means, now known or hereafter invented, including xerography, photocopying and recording, or in any information storage or retrieval system, is forbidden without the written permission of the editorial office, Silhouette Books, 300 East 42nd Street, New York, NY 10017 U.S.A.

All characters in this book have no existence outside the imagination of the author and have no relation whatsoever to anyone bearing the same name or names. They are not even distantly inspired by any individual known or unknown to the author, and all incidents are pure invention.

This edition published by arrangement with Harlequin Books S.A.

® and TM are trademarks of Harlequin Books S.A., used under license. Trademarks indicated with ® are registered in the United States Patent and Trademark Office, the Canadian Trade Marks Office and in other countries.

Visit Silhouette at www.eHarlequin.com

Printed in U.S.A.

Books by Carol Grace

Silhouette Romance

Make Room for Nanny #690
A Taste of Heaven #751
Home Is Where the Heart Is #882
Mail-Order Male #955
The Lady Wore Spurs #1010
*Lonely Millionaire #1057
*Almost a Husband #1105
*Almost Married #1142
The Rancher and the Lost Bride #1153
†Granted: Big Sky Groom #1277
†Granted: Wild West Bride #1303
†Granted: A Family for Baby #1345
Married to the Sheik #1391
The Librarian's Secret Wish #1473

*Miramar Inn
†Best-Kept Wishes

Silhouette Desire

Wife for a Night #1118
*The Heiress Inherits a
    Cowboy* #1145
Expecting... #1205
The Magnificent M.D. #1284

CAROL GRACE

has always been interested in travel and living abroad.
She spent her junior year in college in France and toured
the world working on the hospital ship HOPE. She and
her husband spent the first year and a half of their marriage in Iran, where they both taught English. Then, with
their toddler daughter, they lived in Algeria for two
years.

Carol says that writing is another way of making her life
exciting. Her office is her mountaintop home, which
overlooks the Pacific Ocean and which she shares with
her inventor husband, their daughter, who just graduated
college, and their teenage son.

IT'S OUR 20th ANNIVERSARY!
We'll be celebrating all year,
Continuing with these fabulous titles,
On sale in September 2000.

Intimate Moments

 #1027 Night Shield
Nora Roberts

#1028 Night of No Return
Eileen Wilks

 #1029 Cinderella for a Night
Susan Mallery

#1030 I'll Be Seeing You
Beverly Bird

#1031 Bluer Than Velvet
Mary McBride

#1032 The Temptation of Sean MacNeill
Virginia Kantra

Special Edition

#1345 The M.D. She Had To Marry
Christine Rimmer

#1346 Father Most Wanted
Marie Ferrarella

#1347 Gray Wolf's Woman
Peggy Webb

#1348 For His Little Girl
Lucy Gordon

#1349 A Child on the Way
Janis Reams Hudson

 #1350 At the Heart's Command
Patricia McLinn

Desire

 #1315 Slow Waltz Across Texas
Peggy Moreland

 #1316 Rock Solid
Jennifer Greene

#1317 The Next Santini Bride
Maureen Child

 #1318 Mail-Order Cinderella
Kathryn Jensen

#1319 Lady with a Past
Ryanne Corey

#1320 Doctor for Keeps
Kristi Gold

Romance

#1468 His Expectant Neighbor
Susan Meier

#1469 Marrying Maddy
Kasey Michaels

#1470 Daddy in Dress Blues
Cathie Linz

 #1471 The Princess's Proposal
Valerie Parv

#1472 A Gleam in His Eye
Terry Essig

#1473 The Librarian's Secret Wish
Carol Grace

Chapter One

He *couldn't* be anybody's father. In a library full of suburban children and their white-bread, well-dressed parents, he stood out like Hawkeye in *The Last of the Mohicans* or the Count in *The Count of Monte Cristo* or.... How did she know he wasn't anybody's father? It was the leather bomber jacket. It was also the hair, a shade too long, and the way he stood, arms folded over his chest, feet planted apart.

It was story hour at the Bayside Library, and the children's section was packed with wriggling, squirming munchkins. Claire Cooper was halfway through the story of Paul Bunyan when she noticed the man. How could she not? He was the kind of man a woman, any woman, especially one who worked with women and children all day, *would* notice. Claire could barely concentrate on anybody or anything else for that matter. While he looked relaxed on the outside, Claire had the feeling that inside he was as tense as a tiger about to pounce.

If he was going to pounce, who was he going to pounce on? Her? She shivered and lost her place. Just for a second. No one noticed. No one but him. He narrowed his eyes, incredible gray-green eyes that seemed to look deep inside her. If he wasn't anybody's father then who was he? Men who looked like dashing figures out of books didn't wander into children's libraries for no reason.

"Miz Cooper..." A small hand tugged at her skirt and jarred her back to reality. How long had she been daydreaming? She looked back at the page, but the words blurred before her eyes. Fortunately she knew the book by heart. After all, she'd been reading it and hundreds of other stories for five years to the children of the same neighborhood.

When she looked up again she noticed the man had moved to her left, hovering over her shoulder where he'd turned his penetrating gaze to the little upturned faces. Now she was worried. Kidnapping and abduction popped into her mind. It happened. Not usually in the safety of the suburbs of San Francisco, but you never knew. She scanned the group. There was a gap in the back row. Her favorite little boy had been there earlier, but now he was gone. Why? He never missed story hour. He'd told her he lived close enough to walk to the library.

She glanced over her shoulder, was relieved to find the stranger had moved on, and read two more stories. Then she briskly wrapped up the story hour, receiving hugs and thanks before the kids all trooped out. It was five o'clock. Closing time. No sign of the boy, no sign of the man. She put the pint-sized chairs on the tables and her jacket over her shoulders.

"Ma'am," he said.

She whirled around. Her heart caught in her throat. He was still there. He'd been waiting in the stacks, hiding behind the reference books. She was alone. And scared.

She straightened her shoulders, asked herself what Mary Poppins would do in her place, then very casually reached for her umbrella under her desk. In an emergency it could be used as a weapon. But not against this man who looked like he ate nails for breakfast.

"I'm sorry, we're closing," she said, her voice shaking just slightly.

"I'll take just a moment of your time." He reached into his back pocket and the blood in her veins turned to ice. It wasn't the usual place for a gun, but anything was possible. He pulled out a photograph and she breathed a sigh of relief. "Ever see this boy before?" he asked.

It was him. Little Andy. The kid who'd been coming to her story hour for the past month. He was Huck Finn and Homer Price and every other spunky, freckle-faced kid she'd ever encountered in fiction or in real life. Only he was special. The way he hung on her every word. The way he begged for another story. Just one more. The way he ran his grubby finger along the spine of a book as if he loved the feel of it. The way he'd followed her home yesterday and explained he wanted to see where she lived.

He'd seemed surprised and disappointed when he'd found out she wasn't married. As if every woman over thirty was supposed to have a husband. She hoped some day when the boy grew up, he'd realize marriage was not the only goal for a woman these days. Even for a woman like her who loved children. She'd managed to have children in her life and a career as well. And there were so many things she could accomplish because she was unencumbered, so many other ways to use her considerable energy—securing a bookmobile for the neighborhood and getting her master's degree, for example—without the distraction of a husband and children of her own.

Claire looked up and met the man's steely gaze, then looked away quickly. He was waiting for her answer, but first she had a question of her own.

"Who are you?" she asked.

"Nate Callahan," he said. He took out his wallet and handed her a photo ID that identified him as Nathaniel Callahan, Private Investigator, Chairman of Callahan Investigations, Civil, Criminal, Domestic.

The picture didn't do him justice. His face looked like it was carved out of granite. In real life he looked the kind of private eye who fought in dark alleys and was pursued by beautiful, rich women. Right out of Raymond Chandler in the mystery section. He was Humphrey Bogart and every tough guy in every old movie she'd checked out from the audiovisual department. Fascinated, she stared mesmerized at his ruggedly handsome face.

"And you?" he asked.

"I'm Claire Cooper, the children's librarian."

"Have you seen the boy?" he asked, a trace of impatience in his voice this time.

"Yes, of course I've seen him," she said, gathering her wits about her.

"When?"

"He comes here all the time."

"I know that. When did you last see him?" he demanded.

"He was here today at story hour. Until...until he disappeared. One minute he was listening to the story of Paul Bunyan, the next minute he was gone. What do you want with him?"

"I want to take him back to the orphanage where he belongs."

"The orphanage? This boy doesn't live in an orphanage. He lives with his aunt and uncle and cousin right here in the neighborhood." There was some mistake. Either the boy had lied to her or this man was misinformed. "Let's say he is an orphan. I can't believe an orphanage would hire you to find him," she said. "Isn't that kind of overkill?"

"Nobody hired me," he said. "I'm doing this as a public service. The nuns are worried about him."

She looked at the picture again and frowned. "Maybe it's not the same boy."

"It is the same boy. I don't know what kind of story he told you about his family. He doesn't have one as far as I know. His mother's dead. He's got a stepfather, but he gave the boy up six years ago and the kid has lived at the Sacred Heart Children's Home ever since. Until he ran away yesterday. It's crucial he come back now because they've found a foster home for him. Eight-year-old kids are hard to place. So you'd be doing the kid a favor if you can help me track him down."

"I...I have no idea how to track someone down. I have no idea where he is," she said. Her head was spinning. The boy she'd trusted, the boy who listened with rapt attention to her stories, who loved books just as much as she had done when she was a child, who'd confided in her—that boy didn't have a family? He lived in an orphanage? Her heart went out to him. If he'd lied to her, he had a good reason.

"You're not doing him any favors by protecting him," he said.

"Why would I protect him?" she said hotly. "I have no reason to do that. I tell you I don't know where he is. I'm a children's librarian. I've been dealing with children for many years, and I think I know when they're telling the truth or not." But even as she said the words, she wondered.... Had the boy told her the truth about his home life? Was she really that good at understanding children? She knew one thing, if that boy was a liar, then he was a good one. He'd even supplied details about how his aunt and uncle favored his cousin and ignored him. She'd identified immediately with his situation. Growing up without a mother, moving from state to state, turning to the local libraries for escape, she knew all about coping with a less-than-perfect childhood.

Claire leaned against the bookshelf, unaware that she'd pushed a reference book toward the edge of the shelf. Nate reached to catch it before it fell, brushing her cheek with his hand. She shivered as his fingers touched her skin and her face flamed. She didn't know what he was going to do next. All she knew was this was the kind of man who made her nervous. There were no men in her life. It wasn't a choice she'd made deliberately, that's just the way it was. She'd grown up with her father on military bases from Texas to Alaska, surrounded by macho men and feeling ignored and unloved. She had her own life in order now, stable and predictable. If she ever changed her mind and wanted a man around, it would not be this kind of man—sexy, good-looking and dangerous.

"Relax," he said, tapping her shoulder with his hand. "All I want is to find this kid."

Relax? When the touch of his hand sent her heart hammering so loud he could probably hear it? "I want to find him as much as you do," she said, keeping her voice steady. "He's a favorite of mine." She braced herself against the shelf carefully, so as not to dislodge any more books, and he took his hand away. She wrapped her arms around her waist.

"Librarians have favorites?" he asked, raising one eyebrow.

"Of course." What did he think she was, a robot? "We're only human. My favorites are usually kids who love books as much as I do. Not necessarily the same books. Not necessarily the best-behaved kids, but..." What was she doing, rattling on like that when he couldn't really be interested in librarians in general or her in particular? "I have no idea where he is," she said. "You're a private investigator. This is your job. Don't you have any leads?"

"Just this one. Sister Evangeline, the director of the orphanage, told me the boy loves books and he frequents your library. She knew this was the one place he'd go. Speaking of favorites, he seems to be one of hers."

"So nuns have favorites too?" she asked.

His mouth twisted into a grimace that could have been mistaken for a smile, but wasn't. "Apparently," he said.

"I see. Well, she's right about his coming here. After story hour yesterday he walked me home. I live right in the neighborhood. I invited him in, gave him a cookie and a glass of milk, and he left. He was back here today as usual. Come to think of it, he looked a little more rumpled than usual, and he was wearing the same clothes as yesterday. As if he hadn't been home.''

She frowned and pictured his wide eyes, his shaggy hair hanging over his forehead, and wondered where he'd spent the night. She wished she'd known he was running away. Maybe she could have stopped him and helped him. "I don't understand," she mused, more to herself than to the detective. "I never ran away. No matter how bad things were. Neither did anyone I knew. Of course I didn't live in an orphanage. And I'm not a boy. But I can't imagine…''

"Can't you?'' he asked. "No, most people can't.''

Shocked at the bitterness in his voice, she studied his face. "I assume that you *can* imagine,'' she said.

"Oh, yeah,'' he said. "I can imagine. More than imagine. Just ask Sister Evangeline. I ran many times. But I never got very far. Every damn time she found me and brought me back.''

His gaze was fastened on something or someone far away and she had the feeling he'd forgotten she was there. She could easily imagine him as a runaway kid. He must have been just as macho, just as determined, and almost as tough as he was now.

She hesitated before speaking. He didn't look like he'd appreciate her delving into his background, but she was overcome with an overpowering curiosity. "You mean you lived in the same orphanage as… as…?''

"Does it matter?'' he snapped, his cool gaze meeting hers.

She opened her mouth to say it certainly did, but closed it when she saw the way he glared at her.

"Of course you can't understand how a kid could

run away, can you?'' he said. ''I know your type. Somebody brought up in a house with two parents, dinner on the table at six every night and a bedtime story.'' His voice was laced with cynicism.

She flushed and clenched her hands into fists. How dare he tell her she wouldn't understand. How dare he decide who she was and how she'd been brought up after spending ten minutes with her. No, she didn't actually run away, but after her mother died, she'd packed her suitcase night after night for one whole year, ready to run somewhere, anywhere but where she was. Of course she never actually went anywhere. There was no place to go. Just packing and planning for it took all of her courage. Just imagining walking out the front door, leaving a note for her father, somehow satisfied an urge inside her to rebel against his benign neglect.

''All right,'' she said. ''Have it your way. I don't understand. But if I never left home it wasn't because I didn't want to. Every child thinks about it at one time or another whether they have a happy childhood or not. The reason I didn't run was because I was too scared. Too chicken. But you wouldn't understand that. Not a macho man like you.'' She blinked back a tear from the corner of her eye. What was wrong with her? Why get upset with someone she didn't know and didn't want to know just because he was so wrong about her? There was no sense crying over the past. The past was over, finished, done with. She didn't even think about it anymore.

For a moment she thought he might bend and admit that everyone, including him, got scared at one time or another. But he didn't. He just looked at her as if she was some emotional basket case and he could hardly wait to put this problem behind him and get out of here.

She studied him for a long moment, wondering if under that armor there was anything but a heart of stone. He didn't care about the boy. He was only looking for him because of an obligation. His eyes shuttered, he pulled out a palm-sized computer and jabbed at it with his index finger. He was all business. She wondered what he could possibly be writing. She hadn't given him that much information.

She looked around the library, avoiding his gaze, not knowing what to say. Wishing she could break the uncomfortable silence. Wishing she could be helpful. Wishing she knew the answers. That was her inclination, to help others, that was her training too, to help others get the information they needed. But her joy was turning kids on to books. That's what she'd done with little Andy. She tried to reconstruct the scene that afternoon.

"I remember," she said anxious to say something...anything. "Andy was sitting there in the back row and the next time I looked, he was gone." She glanced around at the shelves and the drawers and the empty chairs and silent computers as if he might be hiding there somewhere.

Nate looked up from his small computer screen as if he'd forgotten she was there. "That's a big help," he said dryly. "Thanks."

"Do you think he could have recognized you and taken off when he saw you?" she asked.

"I don't know him and he doesn't know me," Nate said brusquely.

"You say he's lived at the orphanage for years?" Claire said.

"Since he was two," Nate said.

"Then why leave now? Why run away yesterday? You ought to have some insight, as a private investigator."

"I have no idea. I only know why *I* ran." He gave her a look that clearly said it was none of her business and wild horses couldn't drag it out of him. Then after a pause he shrugged and reluctantly continued. "Why does anyone run? I was looking for my family. My real family. The one I never had. Like an idiot I was convinced they were out there somewhere." He gave a short laugh that was devoid of all humor.

She smiled faintly. "Like Annie," she said.

"Sister Evangeline was nothing like Miss Hannigan. The nun is tough, but she's fair. Without her I'd be in jail now. I owe her big time. Which is why I'm here, looking for the kid. You want to know why he ran, why now? My gut feeling is it's this deal with the foster parents. As far as I know he's been happy at the orphanage."

"Happy at an orphanage?" she asked incredulously. "It sounds dismal."

"Compared to what?" he asked. "Compared to a loving two-parent home, yes. But we didn't all have that option. Some of us were happy to find ourselves under the care of Sister Evangeline, or we damn well should have been. All it takes is one foster home where nobody wants you and you're treated like hired help instead of a kid to make you appreciate a place like Sacred Heart Children's Home."

His eyes narrowed, his voice was flat and unemotional, but underneath she felt a long-buried pain and distress. She didn't want to pry any further, she didn't really want to know any more about him, because the more she knew the more she wanted to know. She was on page one with this man. She wanted to read the whole book. Find out what really happened to him. How he got from A to Z. But getting to know a tough, savvy private investigator was not on her agenda. She just wanted to help him find the boy and bring him back if she could.

"Why can't he stay at the orphanage?" she asked. "If it's so nice?"

"Sister Evangeline tells me there's a cut-off age now. The orphanage is overflowing with babies and little kids. The board of directors have mandated that the older kids be placed in foster care. It's not the only children's home doing that. That's the trend in child care these days. When I was a kid...never mind. That has nothing to do with anything. But if you'd seen this couple...."

"What couple?" she asked.

"The foster parents waiting outside Sister's office when I was there this morning. If you'd seen them, you'd run too. I could be wrong but I got some bad vibes just looking at them. Maybe the kid did too. Maybe that's why I agreed to help find him. That and I owe the good sister big time."

Claire gripped the edge of a bookshelf. "Wait a minute. You're looking for this boy so you can bring him back to the orphanage where he can't stay because he's too old. So in effect, you're going to bring him back so he can go live with these people you got bad vibes from. I don't like this. I don't like it at all. He deserves better than this."

"So do a lot of kids. He's not the only one who'd be living with people who don't want him. Not by a long shot. What are you going to do about it? Adopt him yourself? I don't think so. Don't get excited," he continued. "I could be dead wrong. They tell me some foster families are fine. People who share their homes without thinking of what they're getting out of it. Let's hope I'm wrong about these people. First I have to find the kid. Second I'll have my office check out this foster family. After that I'll figure out what to do. Find another family if necessary. Now, are you with me?"

"What can I do? I'm just a librarian. You're the P.I. You must have ways of finding people. Operatives in the back alleys you can contact."

Nate looked at her as if she was an escapee from a loony bin. "You've been reading too many books. The life of a private investigator is not what you think it is. Or what it was when I got started."

Claire bit her lip to keep from asking what it was like then. He wouldn't tell her if she did. So why bother?

"These days it involves a lot of Internet searches—that would be utterly useless in this case," he continued. "I don't know where else to look for him."

"Neither do I." She glanced at the clock and tucked an errant strand of hair back into the knot at the nape of her neck "In any case, he's not here, and I'm locking up now."

She looked over Nate's shoulder through the window. Shadows were falling across the lawn in front of the building. The wind blew the branches of the white birch, scattering leaves. Missing since yesterday. Where had the boy spent last night? Where would he spend the night tonight? Maybe he'd come back to her house. What would she do if he did? Feed him? Shelter him? Protect him? Adopt him? No, of course not. She had no room in her life for an orphan. Even if she did, she didn't know how to be a mother. She'd never really known her own mother. But her instincts told her that if it were her son who was missing, she'd be frantic. She'd be asking herself, where he was? Why he had run away.

"If you'll excuse me, it's past closing time," she said stiffly. She reached for the light switch but he caught her arm in midair and gripped it tightly. She gasped. What did he want with her?

"Look, Ms. Cooper, I'm a busy man and you're a busy woman. I've taken up your time, I know that. But I have to find this kid. I'm *going* to find the kid. If he came to your library yesterday and went to your house afterward, ate cookies and drank milk, then maybe he'll come back for more today. Close up and we'll go to your house. Chances are he'll be there."

"Not if he sees you."

"He doesn't know me. Didn't I tell you that?"

"Then why did he leave today when you arrived? If he doesn't know you, he knows what you represent. He's very street-smart."

"So I hear," he muttered.

"Why don't you let me handle this," she said. "If he does come to my house, I'll give you a call and you can come and get him." She didn't want this man hanging around her house. What would she do with him while they waited? What would they talk about besides the boy? She'd already told him more about herself than she wanted to, and he was obviously uncomfortable talking about himself.

So they'd both had unhappy childhoods as well as Andy, the orphan boy, but that was it. They had nothing in common other than the fact that they'd both overcome adversity and made something of themselves. Like most people, she'd gotten on with her life and so had he. They were both unmarried and child-less.

Now why did she think that? He'd never said whether he was married or not.

If Andy was still out there somewhere, alone and frightened, he needed her. She'd talk to the boy, get him to tell her the truth, call Nate and they'd both take him back to the orphanage. And if the foster parents turned out to be unworthy, she'd...well, she didn't know what she'd do, but she'd think of something. Or maybe Nate would.

"I'm going to your house," he said firmly and followed her out the front door.

"Oh, all right," she said with a resigned sigh, recognizing the uncompromising tone of his voice. "Come to my house. But you can't come in. You'll have to wait in your car and watch for him. If he sneaks in somehow, I'll signal you."

"You can call me." He thrust a card in her hand. "That's my cell phone number."

She looked down at the card then back at him. "I'll try," she said.

"Don't try, do it." Nate had spent all day on this project, and though he felt he was getting close, he wasn't there yet. He'd hoped the librarian would be more help. Strange woman. She looked exactly the way he'd expected, with her oversized cotton shirt buttoned up to the chin, her straight brown hair pinned back from her face, a few tendrils pried loose as if they were trying to escape. What surprised him was how much she cared about the kid. She'd even looked like she was going to cry at one point. Sure, he'd like to save the boy from the foster home too. But what were they going to do with the kid, when they found him? *If* they found him. They *had* to find him.

Claire Cooper obviously liked the kid and didn't want to see him out on the street. But he'd sure had to spend a hell of a time convincing her to help him out. Stubborn. She was one stubborn woman. He'd been called stubborn himself, more than once. How else could he have survived his own childhood? He wondered what had prompted her to think about running away. He'd probably never know, but that was for the best. He was not interested in uncovering the details of the librarian's past.

"I'll follow you home. That's my car," he said, pointing to his Porsche.

"I have my bicycle," she said primly as she locked the door behind them.

He should have known. He'd never been one to frequent libraries, but somehow he knew they'd smell slightly musty and that the librarian would be stiff and shy and opinionated and would ride a bicycle. Forcing himself to idle his high-powered engine along suburban streets, he kept her in sight as she pedaled home.

One thing he didn't expect—that the librarian would have soft brown eyes under arched brows. Eyes that first looked at him with distrust from behind her glasses. And a stubborn chin that told him she couldn't be pushed around. She was gutsy, standing up to him for the boy, he'd give her that.

He thought he understood her. Her desire to run away from home. Her wish to save the kid from life in an orphanage. She was a woman who devoted herself to kids and books. Probably lived alone. Wasn't likely to get married if he was any judge of people. He understood that. He didn't intend to get married either. It ran in the family. His father hadn't married his mother. Neither was interested in raising a child like him. Both of them were dead now.

Yes, he knew what it was like to be an orphan and at the mercy of the system. He just had to return the kid to Sister Evangeline who would convince him that the foster parents he'd seen offered a better life than the streets. And if not, if he was right about that couple…well, he'd think of something. He had ways of doing what needed to be done and he had a large staff that took orders from him.

By driving more slowly than he had in the past ten years, he managed to arrive at the house at the same time she did. He parked across the street from her small house with the neat lawn and flower boxes under the windows. It looked like her, plain, simple, modest. He wondered where the kid was now. Was it true that his appearance at the library had set off alarm bells in the kid's head? He'd never wanted to be that kind of authority figure, the kind that struck fear into a kid's heart. As a kid, he'd been scared of people like that, and he'd run away. Many times.

He tilted his car seat back, took a drink from a bottle of spring water and checked his messages. There were people waiting in his office, his voice mail was full to overflowing and his secretary was rescheduling his appointments. His admin was doing what she could. And he was sitting on a suburban street waiting for an eight-year-old runaway to show up so he could send him to a foster home. If he was that kid, and he knew somebody was looking for him to send him to a fate worse than death, he'd run too—and keep running.

But all foster families were not like the Cranstons or any of the many others he'd passed through. Maybe the couple who'd agreed to take the boy were really okay. There were ways to find out. It wouldn't take long. He made a few more calls and did a little checking. Everyone said they'd get back to him. Nobody asked why he wanted to know. They just did what he told them. It was a good feeling to have that much power. Especially after growing up with none. Yes, he understood this kid. Maybe that's why he was sitting here instead of meeting clients or putting in some more hours in the office.

After the librarian got off her bicycle and walked up to her front door without a backward glance, he didn't hear from her or catch a glimpse of her. She acted as if he weren't there. He pounded his fist against the steering wheel in frustration. Why didn't she call him? Even if the kid hadn't shown up yet, she could let him know, couldn't she? Why hadn't he gotten her number so he could call her? Yes, he was losing his edge, forgetting details and getting complacent.

Now all he had to do was sit here for hours and wait for her to call or for the kid to show up. As if the boy would walk up to the front door. The minute he'd caught wind that someone was looking for him, he'd taken off from the library today. That was exactly what Nate would have done. If the kid was as clever as he seemed, judging from the lies that were rolling off his tongue, he'd stay away from Ms. Cooper's house. Just in case he didn't stay away, Nate would hang around for a while longer.

As the sun set, he took off his wraparound sunglasses and called Sister Evangeline. He told her he'd just missed the kid at the library, but he had a pretty good idea where he was headed and he'd call as soon as he had him. She said what he knew she'd say.

"Oh, thank you, Nathaniel. I knew I could count on you. There's no need to call the police then, is there? Because he's not really missing, he's just temporarily taken a leave of absence, isn't that right?" she asked anxiously.

He smiled at the euphemism that sprang from her lips. She must be getting soft in her old age. She used to tell it like it was. He rubbed his forehead and assured her he'd find him. Lord, he was tired. All his life he'd wanted to be rich and successful, to be able to thumb his nose at the rest of the world, but now that he was there, the owner of a successful company, with more money than he had time to spend, he found that his daily activities of meetings and more meetings just didn't bring the satisfaction of being out on the street actually doing the work of a private eye.

The truth was, he was sadly out of practice. For example, an eight-year-old kid had just gotten away from him. A librarian wouldn't let him into her house. Five years ago that never would have happened. Five years ago he'd have finagled his way into her kitchen, and he'd be drinking coffee, ears and eyes tuned to the slightest sound, watching for the merest whisper of a change in the atmosphere that would tell him his quarry was nearby.

He got out of his car and walked casually down the street, his phone in his back pocket. Curtains fluttered in the window of the house across the street. Blinds were drawn. Someone was watering his lawn. Dusk in suburbia. He shuddered. He was a city person. As soon as he could, he'd bought a place downtown where warehouses were being turned into lofts, the population was diverse, and prices were still low. He had a huge amount of space, plenty of light, and a view of the Bay Bridge. And while he wasn't looking, his neighborhood had turned trendy.

He circled around the block and went around behind the librarian's house. There was a greenhouse in her backyard and someone was in the greenhouse. Someone in blue jeans and a T-shirt. The kid. Adrenaline pumping, he made a mad dash across the lawn, opened the door and, with a flying leap, grabbed him around the chest and tightened his grip.

Only it wasn't him. It was her. Instead of a man's chest, he had wrapped his arms around a woman's breasts. He was in shock. For some reason it took him a long time to register his mistake and let go.

"Oooh! Ow! Ouch! Let go of me, you…you oaf!" she yelled, twisting out of his grasp.

"Sorry." He dropped his arms to his sides, trying to catch his breath. Either he was sadly out of shape or it had been too long since he'd been that close to such firm, shapely breasts..

"I thought…you should have told me," he said brusquely, tearing his eyes away from Claire's T-shirt with difficulty. *You should have told me that underneath that big shirt and baggy skirt was an extremely sexy body*. Told him? How could she tell him when she hadn't the foggiest idea how her body could have that effect on an average guy with an above-average libido like him.

"Told you what?" she exclaimed, turning to face him, her face scarlet, her lips trembling. "That I was going out to water my plants? Look, maybe you private investigators go after your prey like madmen, and obviously you're accustomed to violence, but the last time I checked I wasn't on the most-wanted list.'' She dropped her watering can and crossed her arms over those gorgeous breasts as if she wanted to hide them. As if she was ashamed of the way she looked. "I told you you couldn't come in my house. That includes my greenhouse. The boy isn't here. He isn't coming here. Why don't you go home?"

"I said I was sorry. I didn't recognize you without your clothes...." His gaze drifted over her body once again. Under those blue jeans were some long slender legs if he was any judge of women, and under that white T-shirt with a picture of a dead poet on it, well.... "I mean the clothes you were wearing," he finished.

"I thought we agreed," he continued, looking her in the eye, "we'd work together on this. We both want to find the boy. We both want what's in his best interest. Neither one of us wants him to spend another night on the street or wherever he was last night. Am I right?" he asked.

She picked up her glasses from the floor of the greenhouse, where they'd fallen when he jumped her, and stood looking down at them, at the cracked lens and the broken frame.

"Sorry about that," he said. "I'll reimburse you of course."

She didn't speak, she just stood staring at the broken glasses.

"What's wrong? Don't you have a spare pair?" he asked.

"I have contact lenses. But I've never really gotten used to them. I...I guess I'll have to give them another try."

"Do that," he said.

She nodded, raised her head and looked at him.

"Well?" he asked. "Are you with me or not?" He thought he had her where he wanted her. She couldn't say no, and she couldn't kick him out if she cared about the boy. But he could be wrong. He'd sure been wrong about what was under that prim, stiff exterior. Besides that incredible body, her hair, though still arranged in a knot, was hanging in wisps around her face, softening the angle of her chin and her jaw. Her eyes without the glasses were a soft cocoa-brown.

He glanced up at the kitchen window, and he knew he had to get into her house. That way he'd be there when the kid showed up. No time for phone calls, no warnings so the kid could run again. Not to mention the fact that he was desperate for a cup of coffee. If he hadn't looked up at the house at that moment, he would have missed the face in the kitchen window, the face of a boy with wide startled eyes, freckles and hair that stood up on the back of his head.

He stared back at the boy. Their gazes locked and he felt like he was looking at himself at that age. It wasn't the freckles or the hair, it was the look in the eyes, half defiant, half vulnerable. Twenty-five years faded away and he could have been that kid. He knew exactly how he felt. Heart pounding like a rabbit's, fighting to keep his fear hidden under a mask of defiance. Adrenaline pumping, ready for flight or fight. Which would it be?

"You say he isn't here, you say you haven't seen him," Nate said calmly to the librarian. "But how do you explain the fact that he's in your kitchen right now? If it isn't who I think it is, you're off the hook, but if it's a runaway boy by the name of Andy, you're in big trouble. I wouldn't want to do it, but if you were anyone else I'd nail you for aiding and abetting, for harboring a runaway and anything else I can think of.''

Her eyes widened. He put his hands firmly on her shoulders and turned her around so she could share his view of her kitchen window. She gasped and then the damned woman slipped out of his grasp and fainted at his feet. When Nate looked up, the kid was gone.

Claire had never fainted in her life. She was the sturdy type, both physically and emotionally. She prided herself on hiding her emotions as well as her body. It had been a necessity growing up. By the time she was thirteen she was five foot ten inches tall, wore size nine and a half shoes and had a woman's body with breasts the same size as now—36D. Public schools on army bases were not exactly the kind of atmosphere where a girl could grow up gradually and innocently. There seemed to be nowhere for a big girl to hide while she came to grips with her passage from girl to woman.

With a father at the officers' club and no mother to help her through adolescence and tell her how to ignore the remarks, assure her she'd grow into her body, Claire had retreated into books, spending her free time at the library and covering her body with oversized men's shirts and baggy pants.

No one had touched her since a certain humiliating and painful episode in high school. She'd made sure of that. Maybe that was why she'd fainted. Maybe it was feeling Nate's warm hands on her shoulders, the shame of knowing she'd looked like a liar, saying she hadn't seen the boy when he was there in her kitchen. Whatever it was, she blacked out for a moment and the next thing she knew she was lying on the dirt floor of the greenhouse, but she couldn't move.

Couldn't speak either. Couldn't protest when the private eye picked her up and wrapped his arms around her. Couldn't scream when he pressed her breasts against the hard muscles of his chest. She opened her mouth, but no sound came out. She tried to push him away, but her arms wouldn't work either. Her head was pounding, her skin was covered with goose bumps and Nate, the private eye, a virtual stranger, was carrying her into her house. When she finally found her voice he was sitting on the edge of the couch holding a glass of water up to her lips.

She sputtered and spat the liquid all over his shirt.

"Good, you're alive," he said, setting the glass on the table, ignoring his wet shirt and her discomfort.

She wiped her mouth with one hand and grabbed the afghan off the back of the couch to cover her body with the other. Yes, she was alive, but she was also humiliated and furious.

"What happened?" she asked. She told herself to play dumb. Pretend she'd been unconscious the whole time. Maybe she had been. Maybe she'd imagined the whole thing. Why else would she feel so dizzy and disoriented?

"You fainted."

"I've never fainted in my life," she protested.

"There's a first time for everything." He brushed his hands together and stood up.

She stared up at a crack in the ceiling, her body still tingling, the blood still pounding in her veins. He'd picked her up as easily as if she was dainty and petite instead of a whopping one hundred and forty pounds. If only he'd slung her over his shoulder, firefighter style, then she wouldn't have to fight off the knowledge that she'd been pressed against his body. That he knew just how big and oversized she really was.

"Where is he?" she asked, sitting up halfway. "Where's Andy?"

"So you acknowledge he was here?" he asked.

"Of course," she said. "I saw him too."

"He's long gone by now. And so are your cookies, if these crumbs on the floor are any indication," he said.

She swung her legs to the floor, folded the afghan and tucked her shirt into her jeans. Her head was still reeling. Even without her glasses she could see not only the crumbs, but the tattered copy of *Homer Price*, the book she'd had since childhood, the only memento she'd saved from a peripatetic childhood, lying in the middle of the floor, open to an illustration of the boy hero. All this in the short time she'd spent in the greenhouse.

Kids had loved *Homer Price* since it had first come out many years ago. But none more than Andy. He begged her to read it to him every time she saw him. Now she understood why it was his favorite. Even though it was old-fashioned and out-of-date for some of today's kids, Homer lived the life Andy wanted to live. A safe, secure life in a mythical small town with a mother and a father who loved and understood him. Homer captured criminals single-handedly. Homer led an adventurous life in the safety net of a loving family complete with aunts, uncles and cousins. What boy wouldn't want his life?

"I have an idea," she said, leafing through the well-worn pages. "I think I know where Andy might be."

"Well, don't just sit there," Nate said. He reached out, grabbed her hand and pulled her to her feet. "Lead me to him."

Chapter Two

Claire shouldn't have told him her idea. She should have known he'd insist on coming along. He was so stubborn, so insistent, so determined to find Andy. And for what? To turn him over to a foster family or an orphanage. There was no stopping him, she knew that. She had no claim on the boy, no rights. Even so.... Oh, he said it was a good place, as orphanages go. But how did she know that? She wished she could see for herself. Just so she'd feel better about helping Nate find the boy.

The detective seemed doubly determined after spotting the boy in her kitchen. He was so impatient he waited in the car while she put her contact lenses in. She was afraid if she didn't hurry he'd start honking the horn, and then what would the neighbors think? Was he restless because his pride was hurt on account of the boy slipping away? Or did he just want to get this whole thing over with? She tried to imagine what it would feel like to be outwitted by an eight-year-old orphan. It wouldn't bother her that much, but then she wasn't a private detective. Thank heavens. She could never go around sneaking up on people.

Claire sat in the front seat of his expensive car that smelled richly of leather and had a dashboard that looked like the inside of a cockpit. She stared straight ahead, though she wanted desperately to glance over at Nate, to make sure she wasn't wrong in thinking his profile resembled the man on the Indian-head penny. To see if he steered with one hand or two. To find out if his shoulders were really all that broad.

She also wondered how she could have avoided this encounter. After all these years of having no contact with attractive men outside of those in books, here she was sitting altogether too close to a man who exuded strength, confidence and success in everything he did, whatever it was. Bringing in criminals or seducing beautiful women. She was sure he was equally good at either. She gave a little shiver of apprehension, and without so much as glancing at her, he flicked a switch and warm air swirled around her feet.

"I appreciate your giving me a ride, but..." she said.

"I wasn't sure your bicycle would hold both of us," he said.

"I have a car. I prefer my bike for short distances. It's non-pollutant, saves on fuel and provides exercise."

"Which explains why you're in such good shape," he said.

Her heart pounded. Heat flooded her face. Good shape? What did he mean by that? She'd always been self-conscious about her size. She struggled to come up with a quick, breezy comment that showed she could banter just like other women did, but she wasn't like other women, especially the kind he knew. She assumed being told you were in good shape was a compliment, but by now it was too late to say thank you, if that's what was called for.

"You haven't told me where we're going," he said, when she didn't respond. "Because you really didn't want me to come along, did you?"

"It's nothing personal," she said primly, clasping her hands together in her lap.

"No, of course not," he said sarcastically. "You think you're going to bring in a juvenile delinquent all by yourself?"

"He's not a delinquent. He's a misunderstood boy. I think I'd have more luck than you. Haven't you ever heard you can catch more flies with honey than with vinegar?"

"That's good to know. I'll have to remember that, so I can use it on deadbeat dads and hardened criminals."

The man refused to take her seriously and that hurt. "Turn right at the stop sign," she said, ignoring his remarks. "That's it on the left."

He pulled up in front of a donut shop. It was almost empty. There was only one man at a table reading a newspaper and drinking coffee. Claire didn't know whether to be relieved or disappointed.

"I guess he's not here," she said.

"What made you think he would be?" Nate asked, trying to keep his voice level and low when he wanted to explode. What in the hell was she doing, sending him on a wild-goose chase?

"There's this chapter in the book where Homer Price takes over production of a donut shop. Just to help out. Because that's the kind of boy he is. It's a very funny scene because the machine won't turn off and there are donuts piling up everywhere—absolutely everywhere—and they have to figure a way to get rid of them.'' She chuckled softly.

"Very funny," he said.

Nate could feel her eyes on him. Without looking he knew without a doubt those big brown eyes of hers were full of reproach.

"Didn't anyone ever read stories to you?" she asked.

The sympathy in her voice really annoyed him. He didn't want her pity. He didn't want anything from her. "That was the least of my problems, believe me," he said.

"Anyway the donut episode made me think he might be here," she continued. "But I guess I was wrong."

"I guess you were. But I'm going in anyway. Just in case."

He should have known better than to think he could go without her. She scrambled out of her car seat and was one step ahead of him when they walked through the glass door. The sugar-sweet smell of donuts filled the air. Nate leaned against the counter and pulled out his picture of Andy to show the woman in the green apron behind the counter, while out of habit, his eyes scanned the place, from the trays of cinnamon twists and glazed donut holes to the vats of hot fat in the kitchen.

A small shape appeared in the periphery of his vision. A small, grubby hand reached around a tray and grabbed a donut. He nudged Claire with his elbow. Her gaze followed his.

She leaned forward. "Andy, is that you?"

Nate didn't wait for an answer. He was behind the counter and had hauled Andy out from the kitchen area by the collar of his shirt before the boy knew what had happened.

When he realized he'd been caught, Andy yelped. The saleswoman pressed her hand against her mouth, her eyes wide and astonished, and Claire put her arms around the boy.

"It's okay, Andy," she said. "We came to get you. Everything's going to be all right."

The hell it is, Nate thought, releasing his hold on the boy and reaching into his pocket for a wad of bills to cover as many donuts as the kid might have stuffed down while there. Everything was not going to be all right until this kid was safely behind the brick walls of the Sacred Heart Children's Home in the custody of Sister Evangeline.

Maybe Claire was right about the power of honey as compared to vinegar, Nate thought, watching her take the boy gently by the hand and lead him to the car. But just in case she wasn't, once he got in the car, Nate locked all the doors just to be sure. For all he knew the kid would make another break at any time. Or maybe that was just what *Nate* would have done if two adults had come looking to take him back to the orphanage. As the two of them squeezed into the small back seat, he gave them a long look in the rear-view mirror before he turned the key in the ignition.

Claire's arm was securely around his narrow shoulders but the boy's eyes were wide with fright.

"I'm not goin' back," he said defiantly.

Yeah, right, Nate thought

"Not right away," Claire said. "You haven't had dinner, have you?"

The boy shook his head and Nate gritted his teeth. Now what?

"I have a pot roast in the oven," she said.

Pot roast. So that's what he'd smelled in her house. Yeah, he knew what pot roast was. That's what they had in those mythical homes he'd never been a part of. What a cheap trick. She probably had mashed potatoes and carrots and applesauce too. Just in case the kid showed up. The woman was cut out for domesticity. Even he, the poster child for a neglected childhood, understood that much. But from the looks of her, she wasn't on the mommy track. She wasn't even on a marriage track.

"No," Nate said. "He's going back and he's going back now."

"Why don't you call Sister Evangeline," Claire suggested softly. "And tell her Andy is safe so she won't worry. I'm sure she can spare him another hour while he has dinner with us."

"Us. Dinner with us? Look, lady there is no us," he said.

There was a hurt silence from the back seat. She apparently had decided not to dignify his remark with an answer. She made him feel like Ebenezer Scrooge himself.

"All right, I'll call her," he conceded. "But he's not going anywhere for dinner. He's going straight back to Sacred Heart."

"No, don't let them take me," Andy pleaded, his pale face lit only by the interior car light.

Claire murmured something comforting. Nate couldn't hear what she said, but he hoped to heaven she wasn't making any promises she couldn't keep. He clenched his jaw and punched in the number of the orphanage. After an eternity someone answered. Not Sister Evangeline, it was a novice. She said Sister wasn't feeling well and had gone to bed early. He left a message that the boy was safe. But before he could tell her he was bringing him back immediately they got disconnected.

So what the hell? How could it hurt to let the kid have dinner with the librarian? The boy looked like he could use a decent meal. But there was no way *he* was going to be sucked into sitting around a kitchen table eating pot roast. Any longings for that kind of family fantasy had been buried long ago. He'd become a realist, first by necessity, then by choice.

He pulled up in front of her house and was just about to announce that out of the goodness of his heart he was going to allow the two of them to have dinner there before returning to the orphanage, when they hopped out of the car and went up the front steps. As if it had already been decided. As if he had no say in the matter.

Reluctantly he dragged himself up the steps and through the open front door. While Nate leaned against the woodwork, feeling like the odd man out, she set the round oak table in the living room alcove for three. He opened his mouth to protest, to tell her he wasn't hungry, that he wasn't part of this party and he'd wait for them in the car, but she and the boy were talking nonstop about donuts and Homer Price and God knew what other unimportant things.

When she announced that dinner was ready, he had another chance to tell her he wasn't eating with them. But it seemed easier just to take a seat at the table than to make a scene. In the meantime the kid had washed his hands and face and combed his hair and looked halfway presentable. Which made Nate think it was probably possible to find a kid like that a decent home. Maybe this was all going to work out after all.

The next thing he knew the woman was reaching for his hand, the kid was reaching for the other. They were bowing their heads while she said a few words of thanks. It suddenly came back to him. That was what they did at the orphanage. A prayer before meals. It was a ritual he'd thought meaningless at the time, but, while everyone else's head was bowed, it had given him a chance to snitch a piece of bread from the center of the table.

He remembered being hungry all the time. Oh, there was food on the table three times a day in the institution. But how did he know what the next day would bring? Adults had a way of taking charge of his life and turning it upside down. So he took food and hid it in his room so he wouldn't be hungry. But he was. He was hungry and afraid. Afraid they'd kick him out. Afraid of being punished. Afraid of being sent away. Here he was holding hands with a kid that could have been him and a woman he'd never seen before today and would never see again. Life sure played some strange tricks.

Catching the kid's eye he knew exactly how he felt. Nervous, wary and hungry. To him this was a dream, having dinner with a woman who could have been his mother if there was any justice in this world. At least she should have had her own family, should have had a kid like him, but didn't. The boy was probably fantasizing that he *was* her family. At the same time he obviously didn't know what to make of Nate. How could he? All he knew was that Nate was the bad guy. The one who was going to take him back to a fate worse than death. The foster home.

"So," Nate said, trying to be friendly, unwilling to play the bad-guy role any more than he had to, "how do you like it at the home?"

"It's okay," Andy said, carefully noncommittal as Claire spooned a heap of mashed potatoes on his plate.

"Have you made any friends there?" Nate asked.

"Nah. There's only little kids there. I'm the oldest. That's why I'm not goin' back. I'm old enough to be on my own now."

Nate shot a glance at Claire who drew her eyebrows together in worry as she passed him a steaming plate of beef.

Nate didn't think he was hungry. He wasn't planning to eat. Didn't want to be part of this faux family scene. But damned if his salivary glands hadn't started working overtime the minute he had a plate filled with beef, mash potatoes and gravy, and buttery carrots in front of him. That's what happened when lunch was a candy bar or a bag of chips from the snack machine down the hall in his office.

"Then a foster home would be the best place for you," Nate said before digging in.

"Uh-uh." The boy shook his head violently. "I heard all about them."

"Could we discuss this later?" Claire asked. "The dinner table isn't a place to argue. If you don't mind."

Nate did mind. In his life the dinner table was the place to watch the news or read the paper while putting something into his mouth. It didn't matter what. Tonight it seemed like the right time and place for the boy to face reality. He had to do it sooner or later. It might as well be sooner. All Nate wanted more than anything was to put this whole orphan matter behind him. The more he got involved with the boy and the librarian the more he wanted to disengage himself. It was bringing back too many unpleasant memories. But there was no way to say any more as the librarian abruptly changed the subject, back to books. What else?

So he ate, not just one helping but two, ignoring the satisfied little smile on the librarian's face as she re-filled his plate. If she thought she could buy his help in solving the kid's problem, she was wrong. Though he had to admit there was something satisfying about a home-cooked meal. Once every ten years or so.

Nate reached for the jacket he'd left on her couch, preparing to drag the kid by the scruff of the neck if need be and take him to the car when he saw Claire kneel in front of the fireplace and strike a match against the hearth. Oh, no. This was too much. A hearty dinner, a cozy fire as the evening temperature dipped. What next? Damned if the woman wasn't set-ting up a card table for a game of Scrabble. He couldn't believe it. She'd obviously seen too many movies. Old movies. Surely she didn't expect him to play. Or the boy. Because if she did, he was going to have to burst her balloon.

"Look, Ms. Cooper…Claire."

She looked up from the game board where she was sorting the letters and turning them upside down. "Yes?"

"I have to be going. *We* have to be going. Sister Evangeline…"

"Doesn't the orphanage allow overnights?" she

asked Andy, carefully ignoring the fact that Nate had his jacket on and was halfway to the door.

"Some other kids go," the boy said wistfully. "But I never had nobody to stay with."

Nate could have sworn a tear had sprung to Claire's eye. The kid obviously knew how to push her buttons. As he himself had known how to manipulate certain nuns. After all, kids had so few weapons against adults. You had to do everything you could, use everything in your arsenal. So he couldn't blame him for the *never had nobody* routine.

"They might allow them," Nate conceded, "but Sister Evangeline has gone to bed so we can't ask her."

"So she won't miss him," Claire said.

Nate heaved a loud sigh. Anything. He'd do anything to be done with this mess. At least for tonight.

"I'll call," he said through gritted teeth. This time he got put right through to Sister Evangeline, who'd already been disturbed earlier by a problem with a sick child.

"Of course he can spend the night with you," she said. "It will give me an extra bed here, which it happens we need desperately tonight."

"It's not with me, it's with the librarian," Nate explained while the other two in the living room waited and watched him anxiously.

"But Nathaniel, we don't really know her, do we? And I'm just afraid he'll run again. Unless, of course, he's with you. You're the only one I trust to keep an eye on him."

"But that's impossible. I live in the city and I have no room for a kid, besides..."

"You'll work it out, I know you will. You were the

most clever, inventive boy we've ever had. You're the only one who could possibly anticipate what our little Andy is going to do next, since you've already thought of every scheme possible once or twice yourself. After all, you were clever enough to find him, weren't you?''

"Well, actually..." He was just about to tell her it was Claire who figured out where he'd be, Claire who was clever enough to find him, when the nun started coughing. She coughed so hard Nate was starting to get worried, picturing her frail body, her sense of responsibility weighing heavily on her narrow shoulders. Then she excused herself and hung up.

"Wait, Sister, just a moment. I can't...he can't..." Nate glared at Claire. This was her fault for suggesting it. In front of Andy so Nate would look bad if he said no. It was her fault from the beginning. But she was unaware of his rising anger. She was looking at Andy and Andy was looking at Nate. Nate recognized the look. Part fear, part hope. So Sister Evangeline wasn't the only one who trusted him to "work it out." It was clear the two of them were waiting to hear what she'd said. And what he was going to do.

"All right," he said to Andy. "You can stay. I'll work something out."

"What's the problem?" Claire asked softly when Andy went to the kitchen for a soda.

Nate sat down and put his elbows on the card table. "She says it's fine for him to spend the night...with me. Not that she doesn't trust you, well, actually she doesn't trust you to think like a delinquent, like me. She thinks he can pull the wool over your eyes. She's afraid he'll run away again."

"But he won't. I swear he won't."

"That's not good enough. Not for Sister Evangeline. It's got to be me or no one. I hate to take him away from here." He looked down at the letters in front of him, at the fire in the fireplace and knew he couldn't offer anything like this in his sterile apartment, even if he wanted to, which he most certainly didn't.

"Then don't," she said. She put her hand on his sleeve. "I have a spare room upstairs for Andy, and if you really have to keep an eye on him you can sleep on the couch. There's no way he could get out of the house without passing you in the living room. If you don't mind, that is. If you feel you can honor your promise that way."

He looked down at her hand on his arm, struck by the contrast of her pale fingers against his dark shirt. She instantly removed her hand and blushed again. You'd think the woman had put her hand on his thigh instead, the way she'd reacted. How many times had she blushed since he'd first walked into her library? How many men had slept overnight in this house with her? His best guess would be zero. He was surprised she was willing to start now. It was only that she cared so much about the boy that she was willing to take a chance on having a complete stranger on her couch.

She wasn't that bad looking. Getting rid of those glasses was a good start. If he had his way the next thing would be her hair and then her clothes. His gaze dropped to the front of her shirt, to the image of the poet in a black-and-white design. He remembered how his hands had involuntarily cupped her breasts right through the soft cloth when he'd grabbed her from behind, thinking she was the boy. But seeing her from the back in that shirt you'd never know.

No, she was not a boy. She was a well-developed woman who, for some reason, was uncomfortable with that fact. She was looking up at him, her cheeks still tinged with red, an unanswered question hanging in the air. He was damned if he could remember what it was.

Finally it came to him. He exhaled loudly and shook his head as he accepted the inevitable. "The couch. Yeah, the couch is fine. One night on a couch can't hurt me."

She nodded, her lips pressed together. She was taking a chance. A chance that he, Nate, was a decent sort of guy who was not going to hit on an uptight librarian. His answer made her eyes shine as bright as if she'd been granted a special favor, when it was the boy who'd lucked out.

The boy came back and the game began. Nate had never played Scrabble before. He'd never wanted to play Scrabble. He didn't want to play now. He had no use for board games. The truth was he'd never played any of them. Not Monopoly, not anything. Another activity he'd been excluded from. Not that he cared.

He wanted to go home and have a cold beer instead of the soda the boy brought him. He hadn't asked for it. Manners. Not bad for an orphan, he thought. Himself at that age? He'd steered clear of adults whenever he could. Adults were the enemy. It was clear the kid liked the librarian. But what did the kid think of him? That he was a villain, no doubt. It didn't matter. This wasn't a popularity contest.

"Are you sure you've never played Scrabble?" Claire asked, as surprised as Nate was that he could put a seven-letter word on the board.

Nate shook his head. Andy had played at the or-

phanage. Claire was clearly an expert. Nate caught on
fast though. It wasn't that hard and he'd always been
a good speller. Not to mention the fact that he was
innately competitive. Hated to lose at anything. He
studied the letters on the board and made another
move. He racked up more points. Andy asked how he
knew all those words. Nate shrugged. He was a self-
made man. Taught himself everything he needed to
know. Had never done well in classes or with authority
figures. The game went on. The boy was staring at his
letters. Nate saw Andy had a chance for a big score,
which he quietly pointed out with Claire looking on
approvingly. What was the harm in helping the kid?
It was just a friendly game, after all.

Claire beamed as if the boy had just won a spelling
contest. The kid grinned proudly and Nate shrugged.
What was the big deal anyway? But there was a
strange tightness in his chest he couldn't explain as he
watched the boy rack up a few points. It must be the
sense of déjà vu. The feeling that he'd been there before. But he hadn't.

The boy yawned. His head drooped. Nate remembered that he hadn't been home last night. Or slept
well wherever he was. But it was clear the kid hated
to call it quits. He was almost as competitive as Nate
was. Finally Claire declared Nate the winner and took
Andy upstairs.

Nate paced back and forth in the living room. He
looked out the front window at his car, waiting there
at the curb. He could so easily walk out the front door
and in an hour he'd be home. Claire would be relieved.
Everybody would be happy. Chances were the kid
wouldn't skip. The way Andy looked at Claire re-

minded Nate of a puppy. He clearly adored the woman. Why would he want to leave her house? If the kid had his way, he'd probably stay forever.

Tomorrow he could return, pick up the boy and take him back. Sister Evangeline would never know he hadn't hung around. No one would ever know. But Claire would and so would Andy. He heard the sound of water running. The boy must be taking a bath. He probably could use one after a night spent God knew where. Nate scanned the books on her bookshelf. They weren't all children's books. There was a wide variety of classics.

He heard footsteps then the murmur of voices. If she was reading him a bedtime story the boy would never want to leave. He pictured him in a real bed in her guest room. Pictured her sitting on the edge of the bed, a book in her lap. Yes, she was clearly cut out for it, but for whatever reason, she was unmarried and childless. There were worse fates, he supposed.

When Claire finally came downstairs he was at the door. He'd almost worn a path in the carpet where he'd been walking back and forth and he couldn't wait another minute. He was going to leave a note, something about an emergency and get out of there.

"Going somewhere?" she asked. Her shirt was smudged, her hair was damp and hanging in tendrils around her face. She'd taken off her shoes and she was carrying a bundle of clothes in her arms. She looked softer, more human, more approachable. Not that he had any intention of approaching her in any way, shape or form.

"Just out to my car. To get something," he muttered. "My shaving kit."

"Oh," she said.

"Everything okay with the kid?" he asked.

"He looks a lot better after his bath," she said.

So do you, he thought, his gaze raking her body from head to bare feet.

"He could barely stay awake for one chapter of *The Wind in the Willows,*" she said. "He's out like a light. I don't think he's going anywhere, so if you want to go home, I feel sure he won't leave."

She wasn't stupid. She knew he was about to cut out. Maybe she even wanted to get rid of him.

"I can't do that," he said. He knew it was true. "I promised Sister Evangeline and I can't go back on that promise. If you knew her you'd know why. It's crazy I know, but the old girl still puts the fear of God into me. There's no way I'd go back on my word to her."

She nodded. "I see. If you need to call someone…I mean, to say why you're not coming home…the phone's in the kitchen."

"I live alone," he said. "I don't report to anyone. Thank God."

"Uh-huh. Well, I'm going to throw his clothes in the washing machine and clean up the kitchen and… and…" She gestured awkwardly and dropped the pants and shirt, socks and underwear. He bent over to pick them up. She did too and they bumped heads.

"Sorry."

"My fault."

She smelled like lavender soap. Her shirt had got twisted and was stretched tightly across her breasts, that were rising and falling a little too rapidly. He had the crazy idea he could hear her heart beating. He took a deep breath and stood up.

"Need some help?" he asked.

She laughed a shaky laugh. "It looks like it, doesn't it?" she said. "No, I'm fine, just a little…"

"A little nervous?" he asked, extending his hand to pull her up. "I don't blame you. Two strange men in the house. If you'd rather I went home…?"

"No, of course not," Claire said, jerking her hand away and burying her chin in the pile of clothing. "You have an obligation and I admire your…your seeing it through. It's true, I don't usually have much company, but…" She didn't finish her sentence. She was out of breath, as if she'd just run up the stairs instead of tiptoeing down. Nervous? Just because a man who'd stepped out of the pages of a hard-boiled detective novel was spending the night on her couch?

She was trying to be casual, as if it was an everyday occurrence. But she knew, and he must know, it wasn't. She'd never spent a night under the same roof with a man other than her father. He probably could tell by the way she was acting. Did she want him to go home and come back tomorrow? More than anything. But what could she say after he'd given his word he'd stay with the boy? He obviously took this obligation seriously. More seriously than anything else.

Of course, she didn't know him. Oh, she knew he was brought up in an orphanage and a series of foster homes. At least that's what he'd said. She knew he was competitive. She knew he was a loner. She knew he was good at his job. But this was only the surface. He, on the other hand, had the ability to see right through her, whereas she hadn't a clue as to what was really behind his tough-guy facade, except, maybe a genuine tough guy.

Chapter Three

Claire tossed the boy's clothes into the washing machine in the laundry room next to the kitchen then started on the dishes. She had tried to deny she was nervous, first to him and then to herself, but her shaking, slippery hands, covered with soapy detergent, gave her away when she couldn't seem to grasp the plates very well. They slipped out of her hands as if they had a life of their own.

She didn't know where Nate had gone and she didn't care as long as he was not in the same room as she was. In his presence she couldn't stop blushing whenever he said something. Was he trying to embarrass her or was that just the way he talked to everyone? Then there was the way he looked at her, his gaze appraising her, his eyes lingering on her breasts. It wasn't the first time a man had looked at her like that, which was why she wore extra-large shirts, but this time her reaction had startled her. Her whole body was suffused with heat. Her nipples had puckered and peaked. Good heavens, what was wrong with her? It wasn't as if he was lusting after her or even admiring her. He was just…just looking.

She didn't hear him come up behind her. When he put his hands on her shoulders, she gasped.

"Need any help?" he asked.

"No…no. I'm fine. Just about finished." Then she dropped a glass and it shattered.

"Sorry," he said, dropping his hands. "I didn't mean to startle you."

"You didn't. I was just thinking…not paying attention." She fished a piece of broken glass from the sink and cut her finger. Oh, Lord, what a klutz she was turning into.

"Let me see that," he said, taking the sponge from her and grabbing her hand.

"It's nothing," she said, tugging on her hand. "I've got a Band-Aid right up here." She reached for the cabinet door. "I don't usually…I mean I'm usually pretty careful."

He pulled a handkerchief from his pocket, wrapped it around her finger and gently shoved her into a kitchen chair. "Sit down," he ordered. "I'll get a Band-Aid."

She sat. And stared at her finger. What must he think of her, fainting like that and unable to wash her own dishes without breaking them? What did it matter? He'd be gone tomorrow, but so would Andy and that made her sad. The part about Andy, not Nate. Having Nate gone would be a huge relief. She could get back to her normal competent self. The self that never blushed, dropped anything, fainted or cut herself.

He unwrapped the handkerchief which was stained

with her blood and wrapped a Band-Aid around her finger. His touch was surprisingly gentle.

"I don't know what you must think of me," she said, staring down at her hands folded tightly in her lap. Her heart was banging against her ribs.

"No, I suppose you don't," he said. There, he was back to his brusque cynical self, thank heavens. That surprising gentleness had only lasted a few seconds and was so out of character she wasn't likely to ever see it again. "Got anything to drink?" he asked.

"You mean alcoholic? There's a bottle of wine I got at the Christmas grab bag last year and never opened. Under the sink. Help yourself."

He found the bottle, opened it and filled two juice glasses. When he handed her one, she shook her head.

"Go ahead. You need it," he insisted. "After all the blood you've lost." He took a drink and nodded approvingly. "Not bad either, for grab-bag wine."

Dutifully she took a sip. It was smooth and mellow and went down easily. Not bad at all. She'd been saving it for something special. That something had never come. Until now.

"How do you feel?" he asked.

"Fine," she said standing up and heading for the sink. "I'll just get my rubber gloves and…"

"The hell you will. Sit *down*. I'll finish up here." There was no use even trying to protest. Not when he used that tone of voice.

What could she do but sit there and sip wine and watch him wash the dishes? It was a scene she wasn't likely to forget if she lived to be one hundred. Six-foot-two, broad shoulders, narrow hips, corduroy pants and deck shoes standing at her sink washing her dishes with a concentration he probably normally used fighting crimes and outwitting criminals. He moved from the sink to the drainboard to the table with the grace of a tiger. Which was what she'd thought when she first saw him. Was it only this afternoon? It seemed like a lifetime ago.

"The person who cooks," he said with his back to her as he continued washing the dishes, "shouldn't have to wash the dishes too. That's what one of my foster mothers used to say. Anyone who didn't agree felt her wrath and had the marks to show for it."

"I take it you preferred to do the dishes," she said, "than to feel her wrath."

"You got that right," he said, rinsing the sponge and hanging up the dishcloth. "Her definition of cooking, by the way, was throwing a frozen pizza into the oven. Nobody argued with that either. Not more than once." He tossed the towel over his shoulder, straddled a kitchen chair and faced her, his wine on the table between them. "No pot roast in that house, I can tell you that," he said. "I don't know how you managed it, but it wasn't bad, you know."

"Thank you," she said. Though she wasn't sure it was a compliment. If it was, it wasn't much of one. "There's nothing to it, really. Just put it in the Crock-Pot in the morning with some vegetables or something. If you can bake a frozen pizza you can make a pot roast. And it's better for you, I think. Of course I didn't know I'd be having company."

Her finger throbbed lightly, less so with every sip of the deep red liquid. She felt a strange peace settle over the house and over herself. A peace that came from the wine and the relief of knowing the boy was asleep in a bed tonight. But it had nothing to do with the man in her kitchen. Oh, yes, he seemed at ease there. Much more than she did at this moment. As if he washed dishes every night, which she sincerely doubted. Probably hadn't washed a dish since those days in the foster home.

She was the only one in the house who was the least bit on edge. The only one who wondered what would happen next. To keep her anxieties at bay she needed to keep the man talking. So she asked about his other foster homes. It was a way of avoiding an awkward silence, and she thought he might have other stories to tell of his unusual childhood. Or maybe she just wanted to hear his voice. Maybe it didn't even matter what he said as long as he kept talking in that deep, hypnotic voice of his. Or maybe she was just plain interested in him.

It was also the novelty, she told herself. The novelty of being the listener and not the storyteller. It was the novelty of having a man in the house. Of sitting in the kitchen drinking wine with a man she'd never seen before today. It was all those things, but it was also just him. A man who lived a different life from hers. Whose voice was deep and rough and steady like the man himself. A man who knew who he was and what he wanted and how to get it. She'd never felt lonely, never felt deprived since she'd left home, but with the house full tonight, she had a feeling she'd been missing something. Something basic. Something elemental.

"Weren't there any good foster homes you got sent to?" she asked when he paused.

He paused for a long moment, and she was afraid he was going to tell her to mind her own business. But he didn't.

"Depends on what you mean by 'good,'" he said at last. "If you mean the kind where the dad goes off to work and the mom stays home and bakes cookies, then the answer is no. But if you mean the kind where nobody takes a strap to anyone smaller than them, then the answer is yes.''

And she thought she'd had it rough. No one ever took a strap to her. The only pain she'd felt throughout her childhood was emotional. She'd had her share of frozen pizzas, but only until she'd learned to cook in a class at high school. Then she'd taken charge of the kitchen, and she'd been in charge ever since. Until tonight, when he'd taken the sponge out of her hand.

She didn't ask another question, she was afraid to. But for some reason, he started talking about some of the families he'd lived with. He was careful not to make them sound too dismal. He made jokes about them, and told the stories almost as if he'd been an observer standing at the window looking in; as if nothing that had happened had affected him much below the surface. She wondered about that.

When he paused, she glanced up at the clock and was stunned to see it was almost midnight. She was even more stunned to see they'd emptied most of the bottle of wine. She felt like she was floating somewhere above her body looking down at a prim and proper librarian and a worldly macho man, like two characters from different novels caught in between where neither belonged.

"Look at the time," she said. "I...I'd better get you a blanket and a pillow. It's been a long day."

"Sorry," he said, abruptly. "I've bored you. I don't know what got into me. I don't usually go off like that." He looked at the dregs of wine in the bottle. "Had to be the liquor. Couldn't have been me."

"I wasn't bored," she said. She reached across the

table and put her hand on his as if it was the most natural gesture in the world, when she'd never done anything like it. "I was fascinated. You know, I've been telling stories for years. It's my job. I have a master's degree in children's literature and library science and I think I'm pretty good at it. But you...you're a natural."

He stared at her hand for a long moment without moving. "Thanks," he said. Then he stood up and went into the living room.

The couch wasn't so bad. He'd slept on worse. But he couldn't sleep. It was partly the wine. It was partly the lingering smell of pot roast, of wood smoke and something else he couldn't name. But it wasn't only the alcohol he'd consumed, it was all those memories he'd expelled tonight. And he'd only scratched the surface. Why now? Why tonight? Why her? Why not keep them bottled up where they belonged forever?

Because...because of the questions she'd asked, the way she'd looked at him, that rapt expression on her face, the look in her eyes that told him she understood. Though how anyone who'd been brought up in an ordinary home could ever understand, he didn't know. Maybe she hadn't been brought up in an ordinary home. She'd said she'd thought about running away. But who hadn't?

In any case, he'd talked for hours about himself and never once asked her anything about herself. He knew nothing much about her except for her credentials. A masters in library science. A storyteller who'd thought about running away but hadn't. A woman who had no idea she was or could be attractive. He turned over and the blanket rolled off onto the floor.

The kid. What was he going to do about him? All the talk about the foster homes he'd been in made him wonder how he could be responsible for sending him to one. He told himself there was no choice. But he could make sure it was the best foster home available. At least he could do that. He drifted off and dreamed of a foster home, one he'd never been in. One that probably didn't exist except in dreams. A big house with a whole raft of kids sitting around the dinner table. The kind of house an orphan dreams about. But not a grown man.

He thought he heard voices. Were they part of the dream or not? Soft at first, then louder. He sat on the edge of the couch and ran his fingers through his hair. He stood at the foot of the stairs and listened. Crying. The kid was crying. Without stopping to think, he took the stairs two at a time.

Claire was sitting on the edge of the bed with her arms around Andy.

"It was a bad dream, that's all," she said. Andy's sobs gradually turned into sniffles. Nate didn't need to be there. He could walk away before they even saw him. She had everything under control. But he couldn't leave. Something kept him standing there even though they didn't need him. They didn't even know he was there. Then she turned and looked at Nate standing in the doorway. Her hair was down to her shoulders, soft and loose. He couldn't understand why she wouldn't always wear it that way. It made her look soft and young and vulnerable. Maybe that was why.

"I heard something," he explained.

"I'm sorry you had to wake up," she said. She stood up and with the bedside light behind her he could almost see through her white cotton nightgown. He was most definitely aware of her slim hips, long legs and the way the soft fabric clung to her full breasts. As if she suddenly realized how exposed she was, she brushed past him on her way out the door.

"I'll make some hot chocolate," she said.

Nate stood there, inhaling the sweet scent of her as she rushed into her room across the hall and past them again on her way to the kitchen, wearing a flannel robe. He couldn't help but think it was a damned shame to cover that body. On the other hand, he wasn't there to ogle a repressed librarian. He was there to keep his eyes on a runaway orphan.

Turning back to the bed, he asked the boy, "Feeling better?"

"Yeah."

So much for conversation. Nate had no idea how to talk to kids. It had been a long time since he'd been one, and nobody had ever taught him how to make casual conversation with anyone, adult or child—especially not a child who'd just pulled the sheet over his head and tried to disappear.

Nate took a step closer to the bed, realizing he'd never even introduced himself to the boy. "You can call me Nate," he said feeling as awkward as a kid himself. "I...uh, I used to live at the home. When I was a kid," he continued. The kid said nothing. What did he expect? That Andy would pop out from under the blanket and ask him what it was like back then, how he liked Sister Evangeline and if the monkey bars had been installed on the playground at that time? The boy was not interested in making conversation. What kid was? The boy didn't like him. Why should he? Nate represented authority. But damn it, he was determined to get something out of him. Something more than a one-syllable response.

"I'm a private detective now," Nate continued, hoping that wouldn't freak the kid out completely. "Sister Evangeline called me when you ran away. She was worried about you. I know she seems strict, she always did to me. But now I realize she really cares about the kids. She cares about you."

The boy slid the blanket down once again and looked at Nate as if he didn't believe a word he'd said. Why should he? Why would a kid like that trust him anyway? Especially being a private eye. Maybe he shouldn't have told him. But one thing he knew—as a kid and as an adult, he hated to be lied to. Always had, always would.

"Tell me," Nate continued. "They still have bed checks at night?"

"Uh-huh."

"Then how did you sneak out?" Nate asked. He was curious. It hadn't been that easy twenty-five years ago.

The blue eyes studied Nate for a long moment, as if trying to decide whether to confide in an adult— always a risky proposition. Claire was right. Andy did look better, clean. He looked fine. If Nate was a foster parent he'd consider taking him. But it was wrong to judge kids by how they looked on the outside, when what was inside was what mattered. Adults too. This kid might have serious, emotional problems. Anyone who'd been abandoned by his parents was bound to be messed up somehow. That included himself.

Nate raised one hand, hoping to assure the kid he could be trusted. "I won't tell anyone, I swear."

The boy shrugged as if he didn't care who he told.

It was a gesture Nate was only too familiar with. It usually signified something like *why should I trust you?* or *don't do me any favors* and *yeah, sure you won't tell.*

"Stuffed a pillow under the blankets," Andy said. "They thought it was me. Then climbed down the drainpipe."

Nate nodded. Simple. Classic. He'd done it himself a dozen times. Only he'd usually got caught before he even got off the grounds. The kid was obviously faster, quieter and sneakier than he'd been. He admired that. Maybe he shouldn't, but he did.

"Where did you spend the night?" Nate asked.

Andy pressed his lips together and didn't answer.

"It doesn't matter," Nate said. "I just wondered."

Andy gave Nate a long, hard look as if trying to determine if he deserved a boy's confidence or not. Nate remembered the unwritten rules of runaways and orphans. Rule number one: *Never give out any information you don't have to.* People will use it against you. People being grown-ups, and grown-ups having their own agendas. Rule number two: *Never trust a grown-up.*

"Do you believe in werewolves?" the boy asked.

"Werewolves?" Nate repeated, startled. He shouldn't have been startled. He should have remembered rule number three: *When somebody asks you a question you don't want to answer, change the subject.* "No, I don't believe in them," he said firmly.

"Me either," the boy said a little too quickly. "But I heard one tonight."

"Did it sound like this?" Nate did a pretty good imitation of a dog howling, if he did say so himself.

"Yeah," the boy said, staring wide-eyed at Nate. "You sure you're not one?"

Nate smothered a smile. "Pretty sure. That was a dog you heard. I heard it too."

"I knew that," Andy said.

There was a long silence. Where was Claire with that hot chocolate?

"You got any kids?" the boy asked.

So he *did* know how to make conversation.

"No. No kids. I'm not married."

"Neither is Miss Cooper," Andy said.

"I know," Nate said.

"Do you got to be married to be a foster parent?" the boy asked.

"I don't know. The foster parents I had were married. But they may have changed the rules since then."

"Could you find out for me?" he asked.

Oh, Lord. It was obvious the kid wanted Claire to be his foster family. What if Nate found out you didn't have to be married? He'd be putting Claire on the spot, asking her to take him in. She liked the kid, sure, but taking him on full-time? Why would any single person with a life of her own do that?

"I'll try." Nate hesitated. He didn't want to raise any false hopes. As an ex-orphan himself he knew the heartbreak of disappointment. It was better to hear the bad news and have time to digest it. "I have to take you back to the orphanage tomorrow," he said.

The way the boy looked at him made Nate feel like the world's biggest heel. Like he was turning him over to a chain gang or a torture chamber.

"I'll run away again," Andy said defiantly.

"Look," Nate said, "the place isn't that bad. I know. Remember, I spent a few years there myself."

Andy turned his head to the wall. His shoulders shook but he didn't make a sound. Nate understood. As an orphan you could never let anyone see you cry. Never show any sign of weakness. If Nate thought he was doing the kid a favor by preparing him for his return, he was wrong. But surely the boy knew he couldn't stay here. Surely he knew he'd have to go back sooner or later. The kid was supposed to be grateful that Nate had given him a day and a night away from the home. What more did he want? Nate knew the answer to that one. He wanted what every kid wants. What every kid deserves. He wanted the mother, father and the happy home. Lord, what was he supposed to do now?

"I was thinking we'd go somewhere first," Nate said. "Wherever you want. The two of us." He said it without thinking. Spending a day with a kid when he was overwhelmed with work? What was he doing?

"What about Miss Cooper?" the boy asked.

"She can come too, if she wants to." Why not? He was in so deep now he might as well go all the way. If the boy wanted her that much and if she agreed, what the hell. She probably wouldn't want to come. She didn't look like the outdoorsy type. He could only hope. He really didn't want to spend any more time with her than absolutely necessary. She was not like any other woman he'd ever met. She had an unnerving way of knocking him off balance. Those big trusting eyes, that innocent blush on her cheeks. He didn't know what to make of her.

"Could we go to the beach?" Andy asked, still facing the wall. "I never been to the beach."

"Never been to the beach? Never seen the ocean?" Andy shook his head.

Nate tried to remember when he'd first seen the ocean. And who'd taken him. But he couldn't. He couldn't believe he could get off that easy. Just by taking the kid—and the librarian, if necessary—to the beach.

"Sure, we could go to the beach. We'll have to stop at the mall for some equipment, shovels, buckets, towels. Have to pick up a swimsuit for me and one for you, unless you brought yours with you."

"And a kite?"

"A kite. Why not? If we can find a kite store somewhere." He'd never bought one. And no one had ever bought him one, that was for sure. But he thought he knew how to fly one. You can learn a lot by watching other kids—kids with dads.

"Water's pretty cold here, but if we go to San Gregorio beach, there's a lagoon we can wade in, if you want. How does that sound?" Nate asked.

"Okay," the boy said, his voice muffled.

If Nate had expected cheers and a grateful hug or even a smile, he was disappointed. The truth was he didn't expect anything except to feel a little less guilty about his role in this job. That was enough.

When Claire came back into the room with three cups of hot chocolate on a tray, she noticed Nate was leaning against the wall, hands in his pockets, his hair ruffled in a way that made him look younger, more human, sexier—if that was possible. Her fingers itched to smooth his wrinkled shirt, to trace the crease in his cheek from the pillow on the couch. All urges she'd never experienced before. Urges that scared the daylights out of her.

This was a terrible mistake, she knew it now. Having a man who looked like this, who acted like he did, under her roof was a terrible idea. It made her want things she couldn't have. It made her want to know what it would be like to have a man in her house and in her life permanently. Someone to cook for. Someone to talk to. Or listen to, like tonight. Someone to sleep with. Just the image of such a thing made her hands shake and the cups rattle on the tray.

She was surprised to hear Nate and Andy having a conversation of sorts. They were talking about the orphanage, about the personnel—including the famous indomitable Sister Evangeline—that didn't seem to have changed much over the years.

She set the tray on the dresser and handed them each a cup. Her hand brushed Nate's and her heart did a flip-flop. He didn't feel a thing, of course, being a man of the world. He was probably accustomed to having women fall all over him. She did not want to be one of those. These weird feelings she intended to keep to herself.

She sat in the rocker in the corner, one she'd bought at a flea market and refinished herself, thinking at the time how perfect it would be for rocking a baby to sleep. Not that she herself was thinking of having a baby, it just looked like that kind of chair. She wrapped her hands around her cup to keep them warm.

"What's this white thing in here?" Nate asked, peering into his cup.

"A marshmallow. I always put marshmallows in my hot chocolate, don't you?" she asked.

"Oh, definitely," he said. "Never have it any other way."

Claire looked up, realizing that he probably never drank hot chocolate, expecting to see a sneer on his face, but there was none. In fact she could have sworn he almost smiled. Not quite, but almost.

Andy's eyes shifted back and forth between the two of them, as if he couldn't figure out what was going on. Well, that made two of them. Claire was just as baffled as the boy. Just as surprised that a big, tough detective was standing around drinking hot chocolate in the middle of the night with an orphan and a librarian. Maybe more so.

"Miss Cooper," Andy said, setting his empty cup on the bedside table and wiping the chocolate mustache off with the back of his hand. "Do you wanna go to the beach with us tomorrow?"

"Us?" she asked, confused.

"Me and...and..."

"Nate," Nate said.

"Me and Nate are going to get a kite and stuff and go to the beach."

"Oh." It was a good thing she was sitting in the rocker, because if she'd been standing she would have fallen over. That's how surprised she was. The boy and the detective were going to the beach when the detective had made no secret of his wish to get rid of the boy as soon as possible? What had happened while she was out of the room?

"So, do you?" Andy asked.

"Sure. Yes. I'd like to go," she said. She didn't ask the questions she wanted to ask. How did this happen? Whose idea was it? Are you sure it's all right with the detective? What about Sister Evangeline and the orphanage?

"I don't got a swimming suit so he's gonna get me one and him too. Do you got one?" Andy asked.

"A suit? Yes, but..."

"I thought we'd go to San Gregorio. I heard from someone in my office there's a lagoon that's shallow enough for kids," Nate said.

She was stunned. What had happened while she was in the kitchen that made a man who wanted nothing to do with an eight-year-old orphan promise to take him to the beach? The answer was nothing had happened. It wasn't possible. What it was was a ruse. Of course it was. A way to get the boy back without his throwing a fit or trying to run away again. Nate was probably just telling Andy he was going to the beach, but planning to head straight back to the orphanage with him. How cruel. But it was the only thing that made any sense.

"Well," she said briskly, gathering her wits about her with difficulty. "We'd all better get back to sleep." She picked up Andy's cup, tucked the covers in around him and followed Nate out the door. After she closed it, she followed Nate down the stairs to the living room.

"If this is a trick," she said grimly, her eyes narrowed, her whole body tense, "I don't want to be any part of it. If you're not really taking him to the beach tomorrow I'm going to be…" She sputtered and tried to decide what she was going to be—furious, livid, upset—and what she was going to do if Nate even thought…

"You think I'd lie to him? You really think I'd stoop that low?" Nate asked incredulously.

"I don't know," she said, "I don't know you. All I know is that you want to take him back to the home. It's your job. You've given your word. That I understand. What I don't understand is why you'd volunteer to take him to the beach."

"He asked me. I asked him what he'd like to do, and he said he wanted to go to the beach. It's not such a big deal. So he needs a suit. We'll stop by the mall. Can't go to the beach without your swimsuit or a bucket or whatever." Their gazes met and held for a long moment, which made her uneasy. She was just trying to understand, now that she finally believed he was really going to do it, *why* he was going to do it.

"You can close your mouth now," he said. "And pick your chin up off the floor. We're going to the beach. Don't make such a big deal out of it. Believe me, it's not that far and it's not that much trouble or I wouldn't be doing it. You're under no obligation to come with us. But you heard him, he *wants* you to come."

But do you? She'd never have the nerve to ask that question. Too afraid of hearing the answer.

"Okay," she said. Then she turned and walked back upstairs, trying to digest this news, putting one foot ahead of the other like the robot he'd thought she was. And probably still did. She opened the door to the guest room and was relieved to see the boy had gone back to sleep. His cheek was flattened against the pillow and his mouth was curved in a faint smile.

She wished Nate could see him, see the smile on his face. See what he'd done for the boy. The promise of a day at the beach. She didn't know why he'd done it, maybe Nate didn't know either. But he meant it, she believed that now. Whether it was out of guilt or bribery or whatever, he ought to know how much the trip meant to the boy. She didn't let herself think what would happen after the beach, after the fun and games were over and Andy was back in the orphanage or on his way to the foster home. One day at a time, she told herself. If she tried to think too far in advance it would spoil the joy she felt looking at the boy who was sleeping in her spare room.

In the morning she took Andy's clothes out of the dryer and made pancakes for breakfast. She fought off the feeling that this is what life was supposed to be like. That this was the role fate had intended for her. Because it wasn't. She was a dedicated career woman. Everyone said so. They admired her for that. She never had to leave work early or take personal calls at the library. She'd devoted herself to her work. She had projects to improve the library, to make it more accessible and more user-friendly, to bring the library out into the community. She had ideas she'd never told anybody about yet.

It was enough. It was satisfying, challenging and invigorating. She got to be around kids all day. She made a difference in their lives. So any wishful thinking of having it all, or changing her life around to include a family, was just that—wishful thinking. And destructive thinking as well. It had the possibility of destroying her well-being.

Nate didn't say much to her at breakfast. She wondered if he was having second thoughts about spending the day with an orphan and a librarian at the beach. If he was, he concealed them under a calm exterior. She offered to pack a picnic lunch but Nate said they'd pick up food along the way. So he hadn't changed his mind after all. Andy, in his freshly washed clothes, barely ate anything. He chattered on about the beach, asking non-stop questions—how deep was the water, how warm was the water, how high were the waves—questions Nate answered with surprising patience.

Claire put her swimsuit on, though she had no intention of wearing it in a public place. It was just that they were going to the beach and that's what you wore to the beach. You also layered a shirt and a sweater and pants over it because it could be cool there, even in the summer. Especially in the summer. Especially at the beach. The San Francisco Bay area was known for its cool, foggy summers. Claire wanted to be prepared. There was no way to prepare to strip down to her swimsuit, however. It wasn't going to happen.

The only place she swam was at the local YMCA on ladies' night where there was no danger of being stared at by lecherous men or being made fun of. She stood in front of the full-length mirror in her bedroom and stared at herself. All she saw was a tall, awkward teenage girl staring back at her. Breasts that were too well-developed too soon. Ahead of any girl in her class. Broad shoulders, a flat stomach, generous hips and long legs. Five feet ten inches of gawky adolescence. She was no longer an adolescent, but she still felt like one. All the same insecurities and worries hit her in the face with the force of a ten-pound reference book on how to survive the teen years. Which she'd barely done.

Quickly she covered her body with the rest of her clothes. When she came downstairs with three large towels under her arm, the boy and the man were waiting for her in the living room. She couldn't believe Nate was serious about buying the boy a swimsuit. It wasn't that he couldn't afford to buy it for him—a detective with his own agency was most likely well-off—it was the time and the effort to go into a shopping mall on a Saturday morning. You didn't find many men there, that was for sure. The point was, when would Andy ever use a swimsuit again? The stories Nate had told about foster homes rarely included a day at the country-club pool or even a trip to the YMCA or the beach.

But she didn't say a word. Not even after they found a parking place and Nate asked to take Andy to the boy's department on his own, claiming this was a "man's business." She even managed to keep her mouth shut when the two of them finally emerged a half-hour later weighted down with purchases.

"The kid needed some things," Nate muttered to Claire in answer to her raised eyebrows at the sight of all the shopping bags.

"What about the swimsuit?" she asked.

"He's wearing it. What about yours?" he asked casually.

"I'm wearing it, but I don't think…"

"I do. I think it's going to be warm today." He looked at the sky. Sure enough, there was no sign of fog, just a light breeze and the sun shining from a cloudless sky. She felt a wave of apprehension wash over her, bigger and more frightening than any waves at the beach, and they weren't even near the shore yet. She told herself there was no way she was going to get down to her suit. Then why had she bothered to wear it? What was she trying to prove?

San Gregorio beach was located about fifty miles south of San Francisco, but only a half hour from the suburb where Claire lived. Nevertheless she was almost as much of a stranger to the wide sand, crashing waves and salt smell as the other two. She couldn't remember the last time she'd been there. There was no reason she couldn't come. She had a car. It's just that it didn't seem as much fun alone. Not with families lugging coolers full of soft drinks and Frisbees to toss around.

The beaches of her childhood were the ones in Guam where her father'd been stationed for two years. Not that he had ever taken her to the beach on his own. But there were military family picnics and volleyball games on the white sand that everyone had gone to. Adults and kids too. Kids to play with. Other people's mothers who were especially kind to her after her mother died. There were some good times. There were some happy memories.

Andy didn't seem to mind not having any kids to play with today. In his new navy blue swim shorts with a famous sports logo, which had probably cost more than his whole wardrobe, he ran to the water's edge and screamed delightedly as the waves crashed and sprayed him with cold salt water. Then he ran back to the towel as if to make sure they were still there, then back to the water. Claire watched him with mixed feelings. He was too thin and too pale. He needed not just one day at the beach in the sun, not just one overnight with someone who cared for him, he needed a whole lifetime of these experiences. It pained her not to know how he was going to get what he needed.

"What's wrong?" Nate asked. He'd stripped down to his swimsuit, tossing his shirt aside, exposing a well-muscled chest with a dusting of dark hair. Not that Claire had been paying attention. She'd done everything she could to keep from staring at him, keeping her eyes on the boy, the shore, the waves, anything but the man next to her who was lying on his side, his elbow in the sand, his head turned toward her. "Sorry you came?" he asked.

"No, it's wonderful. He's having a great time."

"Are you?"

"Yes. Absolutely." What else could she say? That there were butterflies in her stomach because she'd never been this close to a half-naked man? That she was afraid to have too good a time for fear it wouldn't last? That the return to real life would be too much of a letdown, both for her and for Andy?

"Are you cold?" he asked. She felt his gaze travel over her long sleeves, long pants and socks from behind his sunglasses.

"No."

"Hot?"

"I'm just fine." But she wasn't just fine. She was sweltering in the bright sun. Beads of perspiration trickled down between her breasts. She longed to toss off her shirt and feel the sun on her bare skin. But she couldn't, wouldn't take anything off in front of him. She'd melt into a puddle first. She would have stuck to her principles too, if Nate hadn't fallen asleep in the sun after explaining he hadn't gotten much sleep last night.

She watched him for a few minutes until his breathing was slow and deep. Then she took the opportunity to admire his body. She didn't have much to compare it with, but she thought he was just about a perfect specimen, physically speaking, with his muscular thighs and washboard-firm stomach. She was fascinated by the way the hair grew on his chest and disappeared into his swimsuit. When she realized what she was doing, where she was looking, where her thoughts were leading and how shamelessly she was gawking, she quickly jerked her gaze away.

All she knew about romance, sex and men, she'd

gotten from books. All she knew about happy marriages she'd learned from reading about them. A dream of having love in her life was just that. A dream. She had to be ever-vigilant to keep that kind of dream from every surfacing; from allowing it to take over her life and permitting her to become dissatisfied. That would never do. It must remain her secret—her secret wish.

Chapter Four

Claire admitted to herself he was a good-looking man. There was no harm in that. No harm admiring him as long as he was asleep. She knew perfectly well that looks were not everything. In fact they meant nothing. It shouldn't come as a surprise that good looks seldom went with a sterling character. Not in her experience. Character was what counted. Not looks. The only kind of man she would ever be interested in was someone who loved books and children as much as she did.

Oh, sure, Nate had brought the boy to the beach. He'd bought him some clothes too, and a kite. But it was clear he was only doing those things to ease his conscience before he took the boy back to the orphanage and on to a foster home. He didn't love kids. He probably didn't even like them. She had no idea if he read books.

She told herself to enjoy the day. To stop analyzing the man next to her. To stop staring at him. After today she'd probably never see him again. She would try not to worry about the boy's future either. But that was not easy. She should just let the roar of the surf fill her ears and the sun caress her skin, if she dared take her clothes off. Finally, secure in the knowledge that Nate was sound asleep, then, and only then, did she quickly peel off her layers of clothing down to her swimsuit and run down to the water's edge to splash in the cold surf with Andy.

They ran up the beach together, feet pounding on the hard, wet sand. They collected shells and put them in Claire's straw hat. Then quietly, so as not to awaken the detective, they fetched the buckets and shovels Nate had bought and went to build a sand castle far enough away that they wouldn't disturb him. She felt like a child again. Except that as a child she'd rarely had this much fun. Or felt so free. She even forgot she was baring her swimsuited body to the world. Among all the other bodies on the beach, no one seemed to notice her and slowly she began to relax.

"Do you like Nate, Miss Cooper?" Andy asked, dumping a bucket of wet sand in front of him.

"You can call me Claire, Andy," she said.

"Yes, but do you?"

"He seems nice. I just met him yesterday. Like you did. Do you like him?" she asked.

"First I thought he was scary, but then I heard he's an orphan, like me," he said.

Claire had no intention of asking Andy why he hadn't told her he was an orphan, why he'd lied to her about living with an aunt and uncle. She had a pretty good idea. He didn't want pity. She did intend to ask him where he'd spent the night last night, but she hadn't had a chance.

Claire realized that neither she nor Andy had admitted they liked Nate. A shadow fell over their sand castle. Claire looked up to see Nate towering over them. She hoped he hadn't heard them talking about him. Claire immediately dropped her gaze back to the sand castle. There was just so much of six-foot-two inches of near-naked male perfection an innocent librarian could handle. And to top things off, there she was exposed in her black, formfitting swimsuit. She had the feeling she stood out like a sore thumb and that he noticed her. She wished she could dig a hole in the sand and bury herself up to her neck.

"Need some help?" Nate asked.

Even as she murmured something non-committal, he sat down across from them and started digging a moat around their castle. "To keep the bad guys out," he explained.

Andy nodded and happily went off to fill a bucket with water. Claire kept her head down and her hands busy shaping and molding the turrets. She knew it was a childish idea, thinking that if she couldn't see him, he couldn't see her, but at this point, she didn't have many options.

"I fell asleep," he said. "Did I miss much?"

"I think Andy is having a good time," she said.

"Thanks to you. I'm afraid I haven't been very good company. I don't know what happened. I never go to the beach and I never sleep during the day. Waste of time."

"What do you usually do on Saturdays?" she asked out of desperation. She had to say something. Without Andy there, she felt pressure to keep talking. She just hoped he didn't think she was prying into his personal life. Did he think going to the beach or just sleeping was really a waste of time? It was none of her business what he did on Saturdays, and she wouldn't have been surprised if he told her so.

"Work. I always have more to do than I can. So I use the weekends to get caught up. I just live a few blocks from the office, so it's no problem."

"It sounds like a perfect opportunity to bike to work," she noted.

He looked like she'd suggested he ride a horse to work.

"I don't own a bike," he said. "I know what you're going to say. It's a non-pollutant, saves on fuel and provides exercise, but I get all the exercise I need at my health club."

What could she say to that? Just a glance and any fool could see the man couldn't be in much better condition if he rode in the Tour de France.

When Andy came back with the water, Nate suggested he fill the moat and found a piece of driftwood to be the drawbridge.

"In England they used to make their castles out of wood, in the old days," Nate said. "But when their enemies shot flaming arrows over the ramparts, like this…the whole place went up in flames." He tossed a piece of seaweed over the wall and made a noise in his throat that sounded vaguely like a firestorm. "When the Normans came to England from France they used stone and that worked better. Which is why some of those castles are still standing. Sand is not the greatest building material, but since it's all we have, it'll have to do."

He went on to name all the parts of the castle, the battlements and the ramparts, the ward and the keep. Then he talked about famous battles between the English and the French. Real battles. Claire recognized them from history books she'd read and she wondered how much Nate had read. Obviously quite a lot. Andy was wide-eyed through it all, soaking the mini-lesson in like a sponge and shooting imaginary arrows and tossing imaginary flaming torches at Nate who was on the other side of the battlements. Then Andy suddenly stopped piling sand on a broken rampart and looked at Nate.

"Have you ever seen a real castle?" Andy asked.

"Yeah, a few. I went to England once on business and they took me around sightseeing to all these castles. I stood right up here in the ramparts where they fire their arrows down on their enemies," Nate said, with his finger in the sandy slot. "When I got home I had to read up on them. Even went to a library." He shot a pointed look at Claire as if to say he was not a complete ignoramus.

"Did you see a real moat?" Andy asked.

"Looked just like this one," Nate said.

Andy nodded and went back to work on the castle, quiet and thoughtful. Claire was astounded at how much the man had learned about medieval history and how interesting he made it seem to a little boy who was so hungry for knowledge, attention, love, food. You name it, the child was just plain hungry. If only he could get placed in the kind of family he deserved. Where people cared about kids and books and reading and history. She realized she was dreaming. He'd be lucky if he could just get a family where he wasn't neglected.

Claire continued to shape and pat the sand while she thought about men and boys. Building castles and fighting battles. Those were just the kinds of things little boys loved. Big boys too. How did Nate know that would appeal to Andy? Was it just because he'd been a boy himself? What else did he know about? What else had he found in that library, wherever it was? Where else had he traveled?

While she wondered she got almost as engrossed in building the castle as Andy and Nate were, so much so she almost forgot she was wearing a swimsuit in front of a good-looking man. That she was exposed for him and all the world to see. Though it wasn't the world she was worried about seeing her body, it was Nate. It was the way he looked at her, his gaze curious, lingering, appraising... It disturbed her. She was glad he seemed more interested in the castle project for the moment than in her.

Only hunger could lure Andy away from the castle. They'd stopped at a take-out place along Highway One on the way to the beach and Nate had got a huge paper bag. Now she saw it was full of submarine sandwiches and potato chips. Back at their towels they spread the food out and Nate pulled some soft drinks out of the small cooler he'd purchased at the mall, giving Claire a chance to pull a shirt on over her swimsuit.

"Cold?" Nate asked, raising his eyebrows as he glanced in her direction. She was hoping he'd be too busy getting ready to eat to think about her. Obviously that wasn't the case.

Since the sun was still shining brightly and everyone else in the vicinity was in swimwear, she felt ridiculous saying yes. "A little," she said.

His eyes glimmered with amusement as if he knew what her problem was and he found her shyness entertaining.

After wolfing down only a half a sandwich Andy ran back to the sand castle armed with straws to embellish the ramparts while Claire stuffed the leftovers into a large paper bag. Nate leaned back and rested his elbows on his towel. Thanks to his sunglasses, he was able to observe her without her knowing. It was obvious she was self-conscious about her looks and wasn't used to being ogled.

He'd almost choked when she undressed in front of him when she thought he was sleeping. Up till then he'd only imagined what her body would look like. When he saw her in her formfitting tank suit, he thought he'd sink right into the sand. Black stretch fabric clung to the most bodacious, luscious breasts he'd ever looked at, a small waist, generous hips and long slender legs. He was forced to stifle a groan of pure lust, which was hard to do while pretending to be asleep. Not that she was his type. Far from it. After all, looks meant nothing. Well, they meant something, but not everything.

He reminded himself she was a librarian with no sense of humor and no life. At least that's what he'd thought at first. He could be wrong about the sense of humor, since he'd actually heard her talking and laughing with Andy from a distance. And since friends had often accused him of having no life either, maybe that was understandable. For people who enjoyed their careers, their jobs often filled their lives, so it really wasn't a valid criticism.

Back to that gorgeous body, which was driving him especially crazy since she'd pulled a shirt over it leaving him only wanting to see more. Why was she ashamed of her body? Why the oversized clothes, the rimless glasses and the hair pinned back behind her ears? Why hadn't someone taken those glasses off before, unpinned her hair and appreciated her body? Or had they? Why wasn't she married? Why was she sleeping alone in that voluminous, virginal white nightgown? He wanted to know. He intended to find out. Just because she was an enigma. A mystery. His job was solving mysteries.

"Tell me, Claire," he said lazily sifting sand through his fingers. "How long have you been a librarian?"

She stood and started shaking the sand out of her towel and he had a long, unobstructed view of her legs before she answered. "Eight years. Five in the children's library," she said.

"You must like kids to be around them all day."

"I do. They're so spontaneous. You never know what they're going to say next. They ask the darnedest questions. How many stars in the sky? Where does the wind come from? Why aren't you married?" She continued to fold the towels, pick up bits of paper and otherwise keep herself busy until he wanted to yell at her to sit down. To listen to him. To talk to him. To give him her attention.

"What do you tell them?" he asked.

"That no one knows how many stars are in the sky, not even me." She smiled shyly.

"I mean why aren't you married?" he said.

That did it. She sat down with a thud on the sand next to him. "I...I don't want to be. Or need to be. We're not in the dark ages anymore. Where the women cooked over an open fireplace all day while the men were out defending the castle. Where they had to have a man to take care of them. Women can take care of themselves. Women can even take care of men. Women have careers. Satisfying, challenging careers. Like mine.''

He nodded and waited for her to go on. She seemed stoked up, her eyes bright, her legs crossed under her.

''Maybe you think I sit around reading stories to kids all day. I do read stories, but that's not all. I review children's books for the library journal. I do research into children's literature. But my passion is raising funds for a bookmobile for the other side of town that has no library. Just think of all the kids over there who never get a chance to read. Or to be read to.''

''Would you be the driver or the reader?'' he asked.

''Both, if they'd let me. So how could I have time for marriage and a family? I'm like you. I work on the weekends too. I write proposals. I go through catalogues, read book reviews. I go to conferences and give papers on children's literature.''

''All right,'' he said. ''I'm impressed.''

She bit her lip. ''I wasn't trying to impress you. And I didn't mean to go on like that. I just wanted you to know…I mean you asked me….''

''I asked you because you seem to like kids so much. I thought you'd want to have your own.''

''With a job like mine, it's not necessary. I'm around kids all day long. I don't need to have my own.'' She said it with such conviction he wondered if she believed it herself. He didn't.

''I don't think I could stand having kids around me all day long, especially someone else's kids,'' he said.

''What about your own?'' she asked.

''That's not going to happen. It should be obvious. I wouldn't have the faintest idea how to raise a kid.''

''You seem to get along with Andy,'' she said.

"That's different. That's just for today. It seems we have a lot in common. And...I don't know, correct me if I'm wrong, but he seems like a special kind of kid."

"Yes, he is. He's bright and curious and appreciative. And he loves books. I feel like you do. He and I have a lot in common."

He nodded.

"Speaking of Andy, I'm afraid I have some bad news about him."

Her face paled.

"I got a call on my cell phone a little while ago, which is what woke me up. My sources say the foster family that had agreed to take Andy has been cited for taking too many kids into their home."

"That's all?" she said indignantly. "What's wrong with that? That must mean that they really love kids."

"You'd think so, wouldn't you?" he said dourly. "But it seems their motive was to earn more money from the state. There have been complaints from the neighbors, from the teachers at the local school and so on. I don't know about you, but I wouldn't want the kid to go to a place like that. So I left a message for Sister Evangeline. I'm sure she'll agree that the search for his foster family has to go on. In the meantime..."

"Yes?" she said anxiously. "What will we do with him? We can't take him back to the orphanage."

He narrowed his eyes. Where did that "we" come from? "*We* don't have to do anything," he said. "*I* have to take him back to the orphanage. Today."

Her lower lip trembled. She blew her nose with a tissue from her purse.

"It's not that bad, I tell you," he said, trying to ignore the fact she was close to tears. "I spent years there and look how well I turned out," he joked. But she didn't laugh. Far from it. She was trying not to cry but she wasn't doing a very good job of it. He hated to see women cry. Hated it. "Do you have a better idea?" he asked.

"Why can't he at least spend the rest of the weekend at my house?" she asked. "You heard him. Other kids go places."

"He's my responsibility. I promised Sister I'd keep my eye on him. She can't believe he won't try to run away again. Neither you nor I can guarantee that he won't. And I can't spend another night on your couch," he said.

"I'm sorry. I know it's not very comfortable," she said.

"It's not that," he said. "I have to go home and back to work."

"I'll talk to her," Claire said. "We'll go to the orphanage and I'll speak to Sister Evangeline. I'll tell her I won't let him out of my sight and I'll bring him back tomorrow. I can't take him back there, not yet." Her voice shook. He was afraid she was going to cry again. Women.

"You're not taking him back," he repeated. "I am. There's no other solution."

"You'll have to tell him, then," she said glaring at him.

"He already knows."

"You told him?" she asked, her mouth open in surprise. As if she couldn't believe how cruel he was.

"I didn't have to. He's a smart kid. I don't think he was that unhappy at the orphanage. His problem, unless I miss my guess, was going to the foster home. The orphanage is his home. Has been most of his life. The nuns are nice people. They've got good hearts, or they wouldn't be doing what they're doing. They're not making any money at it, that's for sure. When Andy finds out we've nixed the foster family he didn't want to go to, he'll go back to the home willingly, I'll bet you anything."

"Anything?" she said.

He shrugged. "Whatever you want."

She rested her chin on her knee. "Then give him a choice. Offer to take him back or spend the rest of the weekend with us. I know, I know, there is no us. With you, then."

"Now wait just a minute," he said.

"You said anything," she reminded him.

"If you're so sure he doesn't mind going back, then give him a choice, see what he says."

Nate couldn't believe she'd turned a harmless remark into a dare. She'd twisted what he'd said and now she was challenging him, daring him and calling his bluff. All of those things and he was going to lose. He just knew it. If he'd been in the kid's place and he had a chance at another day on the outside, wouldn't he have taken it? Damn right. An orphanage, no matter how nice it was, was just an orphanage after all. Why bother to ask Andy? Nate wasn't sure how the librarian had done it, but she had him where she wanted him.

"Later," he said, unwilling to admit defeat yet. "I think it's time to fly our kite now."

Fortunately he'd bought one completely assembled, because he had no idea how to put one together. He'd watched kids with their dads flying kites at a park, but he'd never actually flown one himself. And he sure didn't know how to put them together. He hoped it wasn't that hard to get it off the ground. With the two of them watching him, he'd better get it flying or he'd look like a fool. For some reason it was very important to him that he didn't look like a fool in front of either one of them.

He held up the kite and beckoned to Andy who came running, bounding over the sand. One good thing, whatever they'd done to him in the orphanage, they hadn't dampened his enthusiasm for life. Or for new experiences. He hadn't learned to hide his feelings. Not yet. Nate hoped he never would.

"That's a kite?" the boy asked when he skidded to a halt, spraying sand in all directions. "It looks like a butterfly."

"It's supposed to look like a butterfly. All it is is tissue paper glued onto these sticks. It has to be light so it can fly. Didn't you ever see one before?" Nate asked.

"Sure, I seen plenty of them. But they weren't butterflies. And I didn't get to fly it. Can I fly it?"

"Sure. Once we get it up. Then you can have it. It's yours."

"Really?"

"You can take it back to Sacred Heart with you," Nate said. He wasn't prepared for the look on the kid's face. The smile that faded in the blink of an eye. The eyes that filled with sudden tears. The way he turned his head so Nate couldn't see.

Nate avoided looking at Claire. He didn't want to see the *I told you so* look on her face. He'd told Claire the boy knew he was going back. He had to know. It was better than the foster home, wasn't it? What did he think, they were going to keep him? Where? How?

Nate didn't know what to say. He didn't want to say anything about any foster home. He was afraid

Claire would say something about spending the rest of the weekend with her or with him or with them. So he picked a safe subject. He talked about kites. He talked about kites being used to measure the wind, to help design the first airplane. He talked about Benjamin Franklin's famous experiment bringing electricity out of the sky with a kite.

"That's why you can never fly your kite on a rainy day when there might be thunder or lightning. Do you understand?" he asked.

Andy nodded. He understood about kites, but Nate knew he didn't understand about the home, knew the boy didn't understand why he couldn't have a family of his own. But he would understand one day just as Nate had. Just as Nate had come to grips with his life, so would Andy. Nate wished he could come up with another scenario, but he couldn't.

Still avoiding meeting Claire's gaze, he grabbed the boy by one hand and the kite with the other. They ran down the beach with the fragile butterfly-shaped kite trailing behind them. It dragged in the sand and he was afraid it would tear. He ran faster and Andy kept up with him. A few more tries and the kite was in the air. Only two feet in the air, but at least it was off the ground. Then it rose higher and higher. He felt his spirit lift with the kite. The kite was outlined against the sky like a colorful giant butterfly.

They stopped running and Nate handed Andy the spool with the twine wrapped around it and showed him how to reel it in and then let it out. Just as he'd seen those fathers in the park showing their sons. The boy caught on fast. He was a smart kid. He needed to be in a home where things like this were going on.

Where someone cared enough about him to show him how to do things, make things.

Nate had known from the beginning he'd never have a father to fly kites with. He was convinced that he wasn't good enough to deserve a dad. He'd been told by teachers and foster parents often enough that he was a bad kid, a troublesome kid. He'd believed it. He'd shrugged it off, but it had hurt. Who knew? Maybe that was what prompted him to be a success. Maybe he wanted to show them all he wasn't all bad. Now he had everything he'd been denied as a child. A home of his own. Money in the bank. Admiration and respect from colleagues. Self-respect and the freedom to do whatever he wanted. He was in control of his life. How many men could say the same?

These days he no longer watched men and their sons tossing footballs back and forth in the park or flying kites together in a field as he'd done when he was a kid. It didn't bother him, he just wasn't interested in seeing the interplay between the generations. The give-and-take. He hadn't had a father and he wasn't likely to have a son. He'd made a life for himself that didn't include a family, permanent or temporary. He didn't miss having a wife, a family, family dinners, holidays, sports or traditions. Not at all. Or he never had.

But seeing the concentration on the boy's face, the look of wonder as the kite rose higher made him wonder if he should have written off fatherhood as easily as he'd just done with Claire. Of course fatherhood implied marriage. His view of marriage was formed by months and years in houses where communication between parents was in the form of screaming matches. He'd never had any wish to participate in that institution. His business partner and his wife were forever introducing him to eligible women but he couldn't see the point in going any further than a brief interlude. If a woman got serious, he got lost.

They spent at least an hour running back and forth on the beach, during which Nate thought Andy was enjoying it. The grin on his little face told him he must be. Nate was wishing he hadn't mentioned the return to the home so soon. He could have waited. He just hadn't thought. When they finally reeled in the kite for the last time, they trudged back to Claire who was still wearing her shirt over her suit, had her legs covered with a beach towel and was reading a paperback book with the library stamp on the spine.

"Time to go home?" she asked. He saw her blink as she realized what she'd said. She was going home. Nate was going home and Andy was going to *a* home. Big difference.

He nodded. "It's getting late."

The three of them plodded up the beach slowly, feet dragging, everyone carrying something—the bag of trash, the towels, the kite and the toys. The air was cooler now. Once in the car Nate knew they'd have to go straight to the orphanage. Any more diversions and it was going to be harder than ever. Harder for the boy to return to the place he'd run away from and harder for the woman to let him go.

"Well," Nate said in a hearty voice that covered his feeling of growing apprehension. "Andy can still come to story hour after school, right?"

There was no answer from either of them for a long moment. Then Claire forced a smile and nodded. "Of course."

But Andy didn't speak. Nate glanced in the rearview mirror to see his lower lip stuck out in a defiant manner, and he knew what was in his mind. Running away.

"Look, kid," Nate said. "We have to go back to the orphanage. We have no choice. But there's one thing, that foster family they had lined up for you... that's not going to work out. I'm going to talk to Sister about it. And she'll find you another one. A better one. That make you feel any better?"

The kid gave him the same look that he'd seen before. A look that said *You don't care about me. You've betrayed me.* What could Nate say to that? Nothing. He was glad to hear Claire pick up the slack and talk to the boy. He didn't say much in response, but she talked anyway, filling the silence as he drove them back. Nate tuned out, preoccupied with worries about the kid, the orphanage and Sister Evangeline. Would she be able to find him another home, or was that asking too much? What would they do with him if they couldn't find anything?

Claire kept up her one-sided conversation with Andy with difficulty. She understood why Nate didn't want to spend another night at her house. It must have been boring at best and at worst—tedious. Maybe if she could just get inside the orphanage and talk to Sister Evangeline, the sister would see she was a reliable, sensible person, one who could be trusted to take care of the boy by herself, without Nate, for just one more day, just till the end of the weekend.

Even if she looked like a beach bum at the moment, with her hair falling around her face instead of in a neat knot at the back of her head, her wrinkled shirt and her pants rolled halfway up her legs, surely the nun could tell she wasn't the type a child could outfox and run away from. In fact, Claire was sure the boy wouldn't *want* to run away from her house. Especially now that he knew that foster family wasn't in the picture.

But when they pulled up in front of the large red-brick building with the high iron fence around it, Nate got out of the car and told both her and Andy to stay where they were while he talked to the sister. Claire opened her mouth to protest, but realized it was no use. Nate was already striding purposefully through the gate and up to the front door. Andy was slouched down in the back seat, with his eyes closed. He didn't have to look out the window to know where they were. He knew, and he didn't want to be there. He shouldn't be there either. He should be with a big, happy family. Every child should.

She looked beyond the fence to the lawn where a handful of small children were playing on swings and monkey bars on a tanbark surface. They looked happy enough except for one small girl who was looking out, her little face pressed against the fence. Claire knew she could never work in an orphanage. She'd want to take them all home with her. Since she couldn't take even one eight-year-old boy home with her, she had to figure out a way for him to find a home to live in. Permanently. She just had to.

When Nate came back to the car, his face was drawn tight, his lips in a narrow, straight line.

"That place is off-limits at the moment," he said as he got into the driver's seat. "The flu. The whole place has it. Half the nuns are sick too and the other half are trying to take care of everyone else. Even Sister Evangeline is down."

"But what about those kids outside there?" Claire asked, nodding toward the playground.

"They recommended that Andy stay with us, if possible. One of the nuns said it was the nastiest flu she'd seen in years. I can't believe it," he muttered. "Couldn't see Sister Evangeline, she's in bed. The kids'll get over it, but she's so frail.... They're worried, I could tell that." His forehead was creased with lines. They weren't the only ones who were worried, Claire thought. Nate was worried too. She would have expected him to be more worried about what to do with Andy, but it was clear his thoughts were with the nun who had done so much for him.

He started the car and drove slowly down the street, still deep in thought. Finally she got up enough nerve to speak.

"What next?" she asked.

"I'm taking him back with me. Back to the city. It's obvious we can't spend another night at your house, so we're going to mine."

"We?" she asked. What did *we* mean.

He looked at her as if she hadn't been paying attention. "We," he repeated. "As in you, me and the boy."

"But..."

"I have work to do. I can't stay here any longer. And I can't baby-sit. You volunteered to take him for the weekend. The rest of the weekend will be spent at my place in the city. I go to work. You take care of the boy. The sister is satisfied I did my duty. I suppose you'll want to stop at your house to pick up a few things?"

She nodded. She was numb. She was going to his place in the city with Andy? It couldn't be. How did this happen so fast? She turned around. Andy's eyes were bright with hope. A distraction. A delay. That's all it was, but that's all that mattered right now. She smiled at the boy and he smiled back. A rarity for him. Whatever made him happy made her happy.

While Nate and Andy waited in the car, she threw a few things into a small overnight bag and then joined them in the car. Just one night, she told herself as they drove up the freeway to San Francisco. There was no other option. She refused to think about the next night and the next. Surely the flu virus wouldn't disappear in a day. Surely there would have to be another solution in another day. But it appeared she didn't have much say in that solution. All she could do was offer suggestions. And this was not the time to do so. Not with Nate looking like he'd just swallowed a bitter pill.

A glance at his profile showed a tense jaw, narrowed eyes and a lined forehead. She was sure this was not the way he pictured the day ending—with the three of them heading toward his house. Or was it a house? An apartment? A condo? A houseboat? He'd never said. All he'd said was that he lived alone. Was there more than one bedroom? Where would she sleep? That was easy. She'd made him sleep on her couch, it was only fair she'd sleep on his.

"I wonder why they didn't get the kids flu shots," she said as they drove along the blue waters of the San Francisco Bay, approaching the outskirts of the city.

"Maybe they did, but the vaccine doesn't stop all types of influenza," Nate said. "And in an orphanage a virus can spread like wildfire."

"What about Andy?" she asked with a worried glance in his direction. "He's likely to get it."

"I won't get sick," Andy said eagerly leaning forward. "I got so many shots. Every kind."

Claire nodded. She hoped he was right.

"When I was there," Nate said, "I remember one time we all got measles. The infirmary was full of sick kids covered with spots. I was burning up. Felt like I was on fire. I only remember Sister Evangeline sitting on my bed with a cool cloth on my face. I don't know how she did it, nursing dozens of kids and running the place as well. She seemed to be everywhere and know everything. I must have been delirious because I thought I saw my mother. But it was Sister. It was always her."

There was a long silence. Claire didn't know what to say. No wonder he felt an obligation to the sister. How sad to grow up without a mother. She felt for anyone who'd done that because she knew how bad it could be.

"You ever get sick?" Nate asked.

She turned to face him, to see if he was really talking to her. If he was really interested in her health or just making conversation. Interested or not, she was obliged to answer.

"Of course," she said. "But nothing serious, thank heavens. My father wasn't very good as a nurse. He'd open the door to my bedroom a crack so he wouldn't catch my cold or the flu. He'd ask how I was and then he'd leave to go to work."

"Where was your mother?" Andy asked from the back seat.

"My mother died when I was eleven, Andy. She was sick a lot and I had to take care of her. I used to cook and clean after school every day. My dad was in the army and we moved around a lot. From army base to army base. I've lived in seven different states. I went to eight different elementary schools. Every year I had a new teacher. New kids.''

"What's it like?" the boy asked. "Bein' in the army?"

"They have everything right there on those bases. Stores, movie theater, hospital, schools and even a library. You never have to leave the base. You feel very safe there." And very claustrophobic. And confined. And lonely. "Some people like it," she added. "And some people can hardly wait to get out."

"I think I can guess which one you were," Nate said.

She'd been so focused on Andy she didn't realize Nate was listening to her. If she had, she might not have talked about herself so much. She usually didn't. The past was the past. She preferred to look forward.

Nate parked in front of a brick building that looked like a warehouse on a street lined with small stores and businesses and more warehouses. He pointed to windows on the top floor and said that was where he lived. Andy toted his shopping bag, kite and beach toys and Claire carried her bag as they boarded the elevator for the eighth floor and his airy, spacious high-ceilinged loft.

"This is a cool place," Andy said. He set his shopping bag down and ran from window to window to look out over the area that was being gentrified with hotels and museums. Then he went off to climb the narrow stairs to the storage area above the living room, glancing over his shoulder at the two adults below, standing in the middle of the room.

"I know you have work to do, so…" Claire began.

"Will you be all right here?" he asked.

"Of course." She looked around at the exposed steel-gray industrial beams, the whitewashed brick walls, the huge computer workstation and black leather chairs. It all looked like a movie set. A movie in which the main character was a well-heeled, single-purpose, single man. She'd almost forgotten what he did for a living. Before her eyes, the image of Nate Callahan, dangerous private detective, was changing to Nate Callahan, executive. Executive who liked the slightly offbeat South of Market ambiance both for his home and his office, which as he said, was only a few blocks away.

"There's a television in the cabinet, a VCR, but no kids' videos, I'm afraid. There's no food to speak of. We'll have to go out for dinner. I shouldn't be too long."

"Take as long as you need. We'll be fine," she assured him. Out to dinner? She had a hard time picturing the three of them in a restaurant. Never mind. This was Andy's weekend, not hers. Her job was to go along with whatever happened and make sure the boy was safe and secure and even enjoying himself. No doubt about that, she thought as Andy came bounding down the stairs, eyes gleaming.

Nate left and Claire turned on the TV to a channel on the cable network that featured kids' programs. Andy sat in one of the huge leather chairs with the remote control in his hand and an intense look on his face as he changed channels as fast as he could click. She gazed at him wistfully, wishing he could always be this engrossed, this happy, always have two adults around to fly a kite or take him out to dinner. She

GET FREE BOOKS and a FREE GIFT
WHEN YOU PLAY THE...

Just scratch off the silver box with a coin. Then check below to see the gifts you get!

7 Lucky

SLOT MACHINE GAME!

DETACH AND MAIL CARD TODAY!

YES! I have scratched off the silver box. Please send me the 2 free books and gift for which I qualify. I understand I am under no obligation to purchase any books, as explained on the back of this card.

315 SDL C4GU

215 SDL C4GQ
(S-R-OS-09/00)

NAME	(PLEASE PRINT CLEARLY)

ADDRESS	

APT.#	CITY

STATE/PROV.	ZIP/POSTAL CODE

7 7 7	**Worth TWO FREE BOOKS plus a BONUS Mystery Gift!**
🍒 🍒 🍒	**Worth TWO FREE BOOKS!**
♣ ♣ ♣	**Worth ONE FREE BOOK!**
🔔 🔔 🍒	**TRY AGAIN!**

Offer limited to one per household and not valid to current Silhouette Romance® subscribers. All orders subject to approval.

© 2000 HARLEQUIN ENTERPRISES LTD. ® and TM are trademarks owned by Harlequin Books S.A. used under license.

The Silhouette Reader Service™ — Here's how it works:

Accepting your 2 free books and gift places you under no obligation to buy anything. You may keep the books and gift and return the shipping statement marked "cancel." If you do not cancel, about a month later we'll send you 6 additional novels and bill you just $2.90 each in the U.S., or $3.25 each in Canada, plus 25¢ shipping & handling per book and applicable taxes if any.* That's the complete price and — compared to cover prices of $3.50 each in the U.S. and $3.99 each in Canada — it's quite a bargain! You may cancel at any time, but if you choose to continue, every month we'll send you 6 more books, which you may either purchase at the discount price or return to us and cancel your subscription.

*Terms and prices subject to change without notice. Sales tax applicable in N.Y. Canadian residents will be charged applicable provincial taxes and GST.

If offer card is missing write to: Silhouette Reader Service, 3010 Walden Ave., P.O. Box 1867, Buffalo NY 14240-1867

BUSINESS REPLY MAIL

FIRST-CLASS MAIL   PERMIT NO. 717   BUFFALO, NY

POSTAGE WILL BE PAID BY ADDRESSEE

SILHOUETTE READER SERVICE
3010 WALDEN AVE
PO BOX 1867
BUFFALO NY 14240-9952

NO POSTAGE
NECESSARY
IF MAILED
IN THE
UNITED STATES

sighed. She'd asked for a weekend for him and she'd gotten it. For now, that had to be enough.

With Nate gone and the boy occupied, she was free to look around. She hoped it wasn't considered snooping, but surely Nate didn't expect her to stay within the confines of the living room or whatever he called that big room, did he? It wasn't wrong to look at the kitchen, was it? No, of course not. Or his bedroom? No, not the bedroom.

When the phone rang she didn't know what to do. She paused in the hallway and looked around. She didn't even know where the phone was. What was a person to do when the phone rang in someone else's house? Let the message machine answer? But what if it was for her? What if it was Nate calling her?

Chapter Five

Claire grabbed the phone in the kitchen. It was not Nate. It was a woman calling for Nate. Claire offered to take a message.

"Mrs. Callahan?" the woman asked.

Before Claire could deny it, the woman continued, inviting them both to a charity event to benefit the Children's Museum, at which Nate would be honored for his contributions. She went on to say how generous he'd been, how much they'd appreciated it and how she'd be sending the formal invitation in the mail but wanted to be sure Mr. and Mrs. Callahan put the date on their calendar etc., this was the event of the year etc. and she'd put him down for two tickets.

The woman hung up before Claire could say there was no Mrs. Callahan and she had no idea if Mr. Callahan would be there at all. But she dutifully wrote the information on a notepad. She knew she should have told the woman Nate didn't have a wife, and if he did, it wouldn't be her, but she really never had a chance. She leaned back against the granite counter thinking how impressive Nate's generosity was. And how little recognition he wanted or needed. According to the woman who'd called, he was one of the major contributors to the children's museum. But no one knew about it and that was probably the way he wanted it.

Then she took a moment to admire the high-tech kitchen with its sub-zero stainless steel refrigerator, granite floors and marble counters, thinking how impossibly homey and dated her kitchen must have looked to Nate. But a quick glance at his open shelves and into his refrigerator showed this was not a kitchen that was used for cooking. No wonder it was spotless. The entire contents consisted of several bottles of an imported beer. He had to eat, but what did he eat? Where did he eat? Who did he eat with?

None of her business, she thought, closing the refrigerator door firmly. Her job was not to speculate on Nate's life, it was to take care of Andy. But Andy didn't need much care. He was watching a program on beetles on the nature channel. She was proud of him for not turning to the obvious choice of cartoons, but not surprised. In the library he'd always shown a curiosity about the world around him. Besides books about adventurous boys with happy families, he'd spent hours looking at books with pictures of animals and asking questions. Always curious.

She was about to join him in the living room when the phone rang again. This time it was a woman with an assertive tone.

"Oh," she said, "I thought I'd get his machine. *Again*. Where's Nate? Who're you?"

"My name is Claire. Nate is at his office. Can I take a message?"

"No he isn't. I've already tried there. I've left messages everywhere. I don't know who you are or what you're doing there, Claire, but Nate stood me up Friday night and I want to know why."

"Oh," Claire said. She knew why. Friday night he was at her house. But she wasn't going to volunteer that information.

"Have you seen him? Is he all right?" the woman asked.

"He's fine. He's been busy," Claire said. She thought that was a safe reply, a bit of an explanation without giving too much away.

But the woman responded with a short, harsh laugh. "Busy? What else is new? I've heard that before. Busy. Too busy for anything but work. That's not an explanation. You're going to have to do better than that."

"Um, well…" She was stuck. Claire didn't know how much Nate liked this woman or how much of an explanation she deserved. But Claire didn't want to be responsible for ruining their relationship, whatever that might be. Maybe a few details would satisfy the woman, make her realize he really was busy—busy working. "Actually he was working on Friday, a case involving a runaway boy," she said.

"Really."

"Yes, really."

"How do you know?" the woman asked.

"Because I was there," Claire said.

"Well that explains everything," the woman said.

"You'll be glad to know he found him," Claire said.

"Well, I'm thrilled. Just thrilled for him. So he found him. Why am I not surprised? He always gets his man or whatever." She paused. "Who did you say you were?"

"I'm a librarian," Claire said.

"Sure you are. And I'm the Queen of Sheba."

"I'll tell him you called," Claire said

"Do that. Have him call me right away. Tell him it's about tonight," she said.

Claire dutifully wrote the message on a pad next to the telephone though she felt foolish writing "Queen of Sheba." She'd expected at least one call from a woman, if her image of Nate as a womanizing detective was to remain intact, so she couldn't be surprised. She was only surprised he'd be involved with such a demanding—and snippy to boot—female. She stared at the phone for a long time afterward waiting for the next call and the next, considering the legions of women out there who fell for private detectives. All of them beautiful. All of them slightly mysterious themselves. All of them needy. But only one called. Where were they all? Why didn't they call? Or was it really true he had no time for a social life?

Nate stood at the window of his empty office, riffling through his mail while drinking a cup of warmed-over coffee. It was good to be back where he belonged. He'd missed the routine, the constant ringing of the phones and the whirring of the fax machine. He'd only been away a day and a half, but he needed his daily fix of income tax frauds, embezzlements and missing persons.

All right, he admitted it. He needed to be needed. But today he didn't know what to do first. There were files on his desk, there were phone messages and there was e-mail, but he was too restless to tackle any of it. And nothing seemed that urgent. His assistant had taken care of a lot of it. He had to remember to give her a raise.

All he could think about was the boy and the woman at his place. How strange it was to have someone else there. That place was his sanctuary. It might not look like a sanctuary. There were no personal effects around. No photographs on the mantle. Hell, there was no mantle. But it was all his. Up to now. Now there were two strangers there waiting for him. They had been strangers up till yesterday, and now they were connected to him in some vague way he barely understood.

On his desk was a memo from his admin. She was working on the foster family for Andy as he'd instructed. She'd been pulling strings, calling in some favors owed to Nate, and had several possibilities. It might take some more time, but she was confident… Nate left the admin a note, updating her on the situation, just in case he wasn't there early Monday morning. He didn't know why he wouldn't be. He always was. But he wasn't so sure about things anymore. Ever since Sister Evangeline had first called him two days ago and turned his life upside down.

He wondered what Andy and Claire were doing at his place, if they were comfortable. He mentally inventoried the kitchen. It only took about thirty seconds. There wasn't much there. No drinks except for beer and wine and, of course, no food. Not like her house where she made a pot roast for one and then was prepared for three. Or thirty. He didn't invite people over. And no one dropped in unexpectedly. That's the way he liked it.

"Hey Nate."

He turned around. It was his partner, Paul. The only man who spent as much time at the office as he did. Which was half of the reason for their booming success as an agency. And the whole reason for Paul's recent separation from his wife.

"Where've you been?" Paul asked, sitting on the edge of Nate's desk.

"You won't believe it, but I've been tracking down a runaway orphan," Nate said.

"Where'd you find him, at the beach?" Paul asked. "That how you got that sunburn and sand in your hair?"

Nate ran his hand through his hair. "Can't put anything by you, can I. No wonder you're the best detective in the city."

"Next to you. So what's up?"

"It's a long story. The upshot is I found the kid but I can't return him yet. So he's at my house."

"At your house? A kid at your house? They must be paying you well."

"There's no money in it," Nate said. "It was an obligation, a favor I owed somebody. How're you doing? Find a place to live yet?"

"Lisa says I'm dragging my feet so I won't have to leave. She's right. I don't want to leave. I don't want a divorce. I don't even want a separation. Never have."

"Then what are you doing here on a Saturday? I thought that's what it was all about, your spending too much time at work."

"It was, but she went out so I came here. I didn't

know what else to do. No hobbies, nothing. The business was all I ever needed. So I thought. I told her I'd change, but she says it's too late. I'm going to do it anyway. Change my ways. My advice to you? Change your ways now. Workaholics make lousy husbands.''

"Who says I want to be a husband? Workaholics shouldn't get married,'' Nate said. "That's my philosophy.''

"Yeah, right. They should just fool around like you do. A new woman every other week. Afraid to make a commitment. Afraid to try to make something work. Afraid to invest in the future.''

"Whoa. Hold on. Is this about me or you?'' Nate said, afraid his partner was working himself into a righteous frenzy.

"No, you hold on,'' Paul said. "This is about both of us. Before you write yourself off as a workaholic and a non-candidate for a long-term, meaningful relationship, I'm telling you for your own good that everything went fine here without you. The first days you've taken off in years. So you're not as indispensable as you thought you were.''

"I noticed, but thanks for pointing it out,'' Nate said dryly.

"No problem. Now leave, get out of here and get back to the orphan. You leave him home alone at your place?''

"Not quite. There's this woman…''

"I knew it. There had to be a woman involved. What else would keep you away from the office for two days?''

"That's not the way it is. She's a librarian.''

"So? Some of my happiest moments have been

spent in the stacks with a librarian. Librarians can be very attractive.''

''They can also be prickly, stubborn, shy, bookish...'' Nate added. But the image of her in her black tank suit, her curves outlined against the sand and the sky came back to haunt him even as he spoke those derogatory words. And sent a shaft of unexpected desire rocketing through him. Attractive? No, that wasn't the word for Claire. She was a candle waiting to burn. She was a firecracker waiting to be lit. And when she was...he wouldn't be around to see it. Because he was going to wrap up this case of the missing orphan tomorrow. Monday at the very latest. And bid goodbye to both the librarian and the orphan.

The idea Paul planted in his mind of a certain librarian behind the stacks of her library, her hair tumbling to her shoulders, wearing a formfitting sweater, her glasses gone for good, her body pressed against his, made his heart race. What was wrong with him? This was pure fantasy. Claire in a body-hugging sweater? Claire doing anything in the library but reading stories and shelving books? It wasn't going to happen. This was all Paul's fault for even suggesting it. He was not going to think about Claire as an object of desire. She would faint all over again if she had the slightest idea he was allowing any such images to enter his mind.

''The still-waters-run-deep type,'' Paul said. ''Watch out.''

''You don't understand,'' Nate said.

''I do understand,'' Paul said.

What Paul didn't understand was that it wasn't that simple. Nate's being a workaholic was not the reason he was not interested in a serious relationship that would lead to marriage. It was his deep-seated and well-founded fear of getting involved. Of taking a chance and failing. It was not having the background, the instincts and the guts to get married. He'd seen marriage from the inside, he'd seen many marriages from the inside, and he hadn't liked what he'd seen. Two people trapped together, forced to take in kids who weren't theirs in order to make money. People who used kids to hold the family, such as it was, together. He wanted nothing to do with that kind of marriage. If there was another kind, and he suspected there must be, he didn't have what it took to make it work.

An hour later, as dusk fell over the city, Andy drifted off to sleep. Claire reached under the cushion of his chair for the control and turned off the TV. She wedged herself next to him, put her arm around the boy and pulled him close. So this was what it was like to have a child. A boy to read to, to share a TV program with. A boy who slept with his head on your shoulder.

She must have dozed off herself, because the next thing she knew it was an hour later. Slowly, carefully she pulled her arm out from under Andy and stood up. She sighed and looked at him slouched in the chair, his tousled blond head against the dark leather. He was wearing the new clothes Nate had bought him, expensive brand names most orphans would never be seen in. She suspected Nate himself had never worn clothes like that. But he did now. His corduroy pants fit him as if they'd been made for him, his sweater looked hand-knit.

Yes, it had been a big day for the boy and for her. No wonder they'd both napped after the day in the sun. But it wouldn't do for Nate to come back and find her asleep. As if Andy would try to leave. Nate had this idea he would if he had the chance. Probably because that's what *he* would have done. In any case, he trusted her to keep an eye on Andy. She wanted to appear alert.

Walking restlessly from room to room, she wondered how long Nate would be gone. He had mentioned dinner, so that must mean he'd be back sometime soon...but when? Maybe he'd be so swamped with work he'd forget about them. Maybe when he returned he'd change clothes and go out with the Queen of Sheba. Which was fine with her. She'd be perfectly happy staying home with Andy.

She turned on the lights in the living room, and went into Nate's tiled bathroom, a small guest bathroom done in dark maroon and black tiles. She washed her face in cold water and pinned her hair back into a knot at the base of her neck the way she'd always worn it before she started doing crazy things like inviting a strange man to sleep overnight and spending a day at the beach. She felt more like her old self, even though her face was covered with a light sunburn. She couldn't remember when she'd spent enough time in the sun for her nose to turn red.

She missed her glasses. She felt naked without them on her face, but she was getting used to the feel of her contact lenses. She had to admit she looked different without them. So different that she started when she met her own gaze in the mirror. She wondered what the Queen of Sheba looked like. Probably wore makeup. Probably had her hair done. Probably wore suits or designer jeans. So what?

Claire would order new glasses on Monday. Everything would be back to normal on Monday. But where would Andy be? Back in the orphanage, quarantined? In danger of catching the flu? Or was he immune? Technically he wasn't her problem, but she couldn't stop thinking about him, worrying about his future.

She went to look out the window. It was dusk and the lights of the city twinkled. The Bay Bridge was illuminated, making her feel like she was looking out at fairyland. She thought for the first time that the city might not be such a bad place to live after all. Shifting her gaze, she saw Nate walking toward the building. He walked like a man in a hurry. In a hurry to see them? Not likely. In a hurry to go out on a date he'd set up at the office? In a hurry to get the weekend over with? Probably.

At the curb, he looked up and saw her. He stood there for a long moment looking up at her. She couldn't move, couldn't tear her eyes away from him. What was he thinking? Was he surprised to see her there? Had he forgotten about them? Was he wishing they'd go away? That they'd never come? In a few minutes it would be dark and she wouldn't be able to see his face.

Maybe it was the fading daylight, the angle of her vision from the eighth floor to the ground, but she had the strangest feeling, as if an invisible cord were stretched between them, a connection that couldn't be seen, only felt. Of course she was the only one who felt it. He was just looking up at his home. As he probably did every day when he came home. Only today she was standing in his lit window looking out. He couldn't avoid seeing her. But he didn't have to stand there like that, staring at her. Her hands shook. Her mouth was so dry she longed for a cold drink, but she couldn't make herself move toward the kitchen to get one, not until he finally broke the connection and disappeared into the building.

"Everything all right here?" he asked a few minutes later as if he hadn't been the man on the street. As if he hadn't seen her since he left a few hours ago.

Claire put her finger to her lips and glanced at the sleeping boy in the chair.

"Worn-out," he said. "I know how he feels."

"Me too," she confessed with a yawn. She tried to be nonchalant, as if she hadn't been the woman in the window staring down at him, unable to look away. As if she hadn't seen him since he left the house a few hours ago. "Did you get your work done?" she asked.

"Some of it. Actually there wasn't all that much to do. My partner and my assistant took care of most of the things while I was gone. Surprised me. All this time I thought I was indispensable. Couldn't take a day off. Thought the place would fall apart without me. But I was wrong. Maybe I need to take more time off. Give someone else a chance to do the work."

"That's what your friend thinks."

"What friend?" He walked into the kitchen and opened the refrigerator door. She followed him.

"The one who called you. Sheba is her name."

"What? I don't know anyone named Sheba." He picked up the message pad next to the phone and read it. "I especially don't know anyone named the Queen of Sheba. This is a joke, right?"

"I didn't think that was her real name," Claire said. "She said you stood her up on Friday night. Does that help?"

"Yeah, that helps. Her name is Diana. I forgot all

about it. Forgot all about her. I bet she was all bent out of shape. Women don't understand that work comes first.''

"She expects you to call her. She said it's about tonight.''

"I'm busy tonight," he said. "She'll understand." He made no move to pick up the phone. Instead, he held out a bottle of beer and Claire shook her head.

"That's all I've got," he said, glancing around the kitchen. "Place looks pretty bare."

"It's a beautiful kitchen," she said. "I assume you don't use it much.''

"Never. I don't need to. There are plenty of restaurants right here in the neighborhood. The designer who remodeled the loft said I had to have the latest in appliances, in case I ever want to sell it. I told her that will never happen. The place is perfect for one person. One person who works in the neighborhood, who doesn't cook and who likes the city."

"That reminds me, someone else called," she said. "To invite you to a charity benefit dinner. You're being honored. I guess you knew that."

"No I didn't know. I don't go to those things," he said.

"She'll be disappointed," Claire said.

"You didn't tell her I'd go, did you?" he asked.

"No, of course not, but I'm afraid she put you down for two tickets anyway. She didn't want to take no for an answer. For some reason she thought you were married.''

"I hope you told her I wasn't.''

"I tried, but…I'm not sure she heard me. It's a worthy cause, you know. They'll be disappointed if you don't go.''

"Then *you* go."

"Me? I haven't contributed a penny."

"It doesn't matter. When the tickets come, you can have them." He opened his beer and leaned against the kitchen counter.

"Did he ever change out of his swimsuit?" Nate asked.

"Yes," she said. "Right after you left."

"Did you?" he asked, his eyes traveling over her bulky sweater and baggy sweat pants.

She felt the heat rise up her neck, coloring her cheeks and forehead. It was a simple question. It didn't mean anything, neither did the way he was looking at her, and yet she was so flustered she couldn't speak for a long moment.

"Yes," she said at last. "Of course. I changed at home while you were waiting in the car."

"Too bad," he said with an unmistakable gleam in his eye. "I liked that suit. You looked good in it."

"I'm afraid it was a little too tight," she said. "A little too…"

"Revealing? Maybe that's why I liked it. Most men like to see a woman at least partly revealed. And most women would kill for a body like yours."

Her face flamed. She didn't know how they'd gotten started on this topic, but she wished she could change it or failing that, fall through the floor. "You don't know what you're talking about," she said.

"Most women would flaunt it, not hide it," he continued as if she hadn't spoken. "You're different." Holding his beer with one hand, he reached out and touched her cheek with the other. "Why?"

She swallowed hard. His touch sent a shiver up her spine while inside she was burning up. She didn't know if he was serious or not. Most likely he was just curious. Maybe he just wanted to tease her, to see what she'd do. Like the boys did in high school. He couldn't mean that about her body. Every time she looked in the mirror she was reminded of her size—too tall, too large, too well-developed too soon.

Maybe if she'd been born one hundred years ago when voluptuousness was in style she wouldn't be so self-conscious about her size, but in this day and age of wafer-thin models, she was only comfortable when covered up. Like now. Only she wasn't comfortable. Not with him standing there in the bright track light from the kitchen, observing her with narrowed eyes.

"Hasn't anyone ever told you you could be a knockout?" he asked softly. "Just let the hair down." He reached for the clip that held her hair in place and removed it. She felt her hair fall down around her face, brushing her cheeks. She was so startled she couldn't do anything but stand there. She meant to grab the clip and put it back, but her body wasn't taking orders from her brain. Her body was suffused with heat. Her hands were shaking. She couldn't do anything but stand there mesmerized by the look in his eyes.

She didn't know what he was going to do. She was afraid he was going to laugh at her, for being so foolish as to believe him when he said she had a body anyone would kill for. Truth was she didn't believe it. It would take more than a few words from a worldwise detective to convince her she was attractive. What would it take? she asked herself. Her mind spun thinking of the possibilities.

"That's better," he said taking a strand of her hair and letting it sift through his fingers. "Next the sweatshirt has to go."

She shook her head, but when he reached for the hem of the bulky shirt with both hands and pulled it up, slowly and carefully, she gasped but didn't stop him. He kept his gaze fastened on hers, giving her time and opportunity to protest. She felt the heat from his body, inhaled the heady smell of malt liquor on his breath. She didn't protest. She should have, but she couldn't speak. Couldn't breathe. Couldn't protest if she'd wanted to. Couldn't stop his fingers from brushing against her skin. From deliberately raising the shirt above her stomach and over her breasts.

Her breath came in little ragged bursts. Her mind went blank. She couldn't remember what she was wearing under the sweatshirt. She hoped it was something, but it felt like nothing. Nothing between his warm hands and her cool skin. His hands brushed the swell of her breasts through the lace of her bra, and she almost fainted again.

He kept his eyes on hers, holding her steady with his gaze. His eyes darkened. She didn't know what that meant. She didn't know if it meant anything. Certainly he'd done this before. Everyone over twenty-one had. Except for her. She was socially retarded. Hadn't a clue what was going to happen next. But instead of turning and running or putting out her hand to push him away, she stood there waiting. Heart pounding so loudly he must be able to hear it. Waiting to see what he'd do next. Wanting him to do something. What, she didn't know.

She only knew there was a longing deep inside her for something she'd never had before. Call it lust, call it desire. Whatever it was, she felt like a wild, reckless stranger had taken over her body. The old Claire would never have let a man touch her. But then no man had ever tried. A boy had once. Only once.

Suddenly he yanked her shirt down and stepped back.

"Hi Andy," he said.

She whirled around, conscious of her racing pulse, her hair hanging around her face, her skin on fire. What if Andy had seen her half-undressed? What if he knew she was lusting after a man she'd only met the day before? What kind of an example was that for a child?

But Andy stood in the doorway looking too sleepy to be aware of anything going on. As she pushed her hair back behind her ears with trembling fingers she went to the boy and picked him up.

"How're you doing?" she asked, hugging him to her and looking into his blue eyes.

"I'm hungry," he said.

Nate looked at the two of them, heads together, one blond, one brown and dark, standing there looking at him, waiting for him to say something. Something simple, like let's go out to dinner. Nothing hard about that. Didn't require much brainpower to come out with a simple sentence but his brain wasn't working very well.

The truth was he was in a state of shock. He didn't know what had possessed him to come on to the librarian like that. He must have lost his mind. Now that he thought about it, he knew where he'd lost it, back there on the beach when he saw her in that swimsuit. The one that revealed so much and yet not enough. The one that made his body react as a jolt of desire hit him broadside.

He told himself it was the fresh air and the plethora

of near-naked bodies frolicking on the sand, but he had no interest in those other bodies. Only hers. Only hers turned him on. Made him want to strip off that suit that clung so tenaciously to her body, to look and to touch and to feel. To awaken her senses, to watch her react.

That was not going to happen. He'd shocked her. He knew that. He'd seen her eyes widen, heard the sharp intake of breath as his fingers brushed the edge of the lace bra. Almost as if she'd never been touched before. Never felt a man's hands on her. He wanted to kiss her. Even now. Even with the kid in the room.

He wanted to walk over there and lace his fingers through her hair and kiss her hard on the lips. He wanted to see what she'd do. Would she kiss him back? Would she scream? Would her cheeks turn pink the way they did every time he did something she didn't expect? Would she slap him? She'd be shocked for sure. Hell, just the idea of it had shocked even him. Up until a few minutes ago. Now the idea was almost irresistible. One kiss. What could that hurt? Everything. It could change everything.

Instead, he said, "Hungry? Let's go eat."

Chapter Six

Nate had in mind the corner restaurant, his second home, where he ate breakfast, lunch and even dinner more often than not. But when he saw the specials listed on a board on the sidewalk—salmon teriyaki, linguini with clam sauce and veal chops florentine— he knew it wasn't the place to bring the kid. Not that they'd mind. It wasn't formal. But at eight years old he would have wrinkled his nose at the sight of a dead salmon and filled up on crackers instead. He wanted to make this dinner special. For the kid. One more day and the boy would be back where he belonged, out of Nate's life. Where *would* he be? Where *did* he belong? Right now he was walking between them, one hand in Nate's, one hand in Claire's. It was a strange feeling having that small hand in his. Nate tried to remember if he'd ever felt like holding an adult's hand in his life. He didn't think so. He felt oddly proud that the kid trusted him. But did he deserve that trust? What had he done to earn it?

"Do you like pizza?" Nate asked.

The boy didn't have to speak. His head bobbed up and down emphatically and he grinned broadly.

"What about you?" he asked Claire.

She shrugged. "Whatever you say."

He'd never been inside, but he'd seen the kids holding balloons twisted into bright shapes standing out in front of a certain restaurant. He knew it wasn't the kind of place the critics reviewed in the newspaper. It was a kid place. The food was probably terrible. But it wasn't about the food. This was about what kids wanted. What this kid wanted.

They got in the car and went to the restaurant. Nate wished he could preserve the look on Andy's face when they walked in the door. Waiters were dressed as cartoon characters, making balloon hats or twisting them into animal shapes and handing them out. Arcade games and video games and shooting galleries and strength tests and prizes. All that before they'd even sat down at their table. It was the kind of place no one had ever taken him. Where he'd never taken anyone or ever ventured into. The kind of place where kids were allowed to shout and run around like maniacs. Normally a place like this would have made his head pound. But tonight he was seeing it through Andy's eyes.

Andy stood in the doorway just looking for a long time. Nate thought maybe he'd made a mistake. Maybe it was too much, too overwhelming for a kid who'd been deprived. These kids in here were used to the scene. They had it all. Parents who loved them, who took them to movies, parks, zoos and museums. They came here for birthdays. Some came every Friday night. The noisy excess didn't faze them.

Andy recovered after surveying the place for about five minutes, and after Nate bought a handful of tickets for the attractions and went in with him. While Claire found a table, Nate took a turn at a simulated race-track game, shoving the joystick around until he crashed the car, then he gave the stick to Andy. The boy was soon weaving among the traffic and jumping up and down excitedly. Nate tucked the tickets in the boy's pocket, told him they were going to order the food and backed away.

He located Claire, and they ordered a pizza, two sodas and a beer. He'd never finished the one at home. He remembered why. In the dim light from the over-head lights he looked at Claire across the table. Damn that sweatshirt. He wanted to see her in something else. Anything else. It didn't have to be the swimsuit, though that was a tempting thought. She was smiling shyly. At him or at the sight of Andy enjoying him-self? Whatever it was, she ought to smile more often. It made her look less like a librarian and more like...like what? What did he want her to look like?

"What?" he asked. He had the feeling she had just asked him something.

"Nothing," she said. "I was just wondering if you come here often."

"Never. It's hardly my kind of place. I just thought he might like it." He tried to shrug it off, tried to sound casual as if it didn't matter whether he did or not, but he couldn't help looking over his shoulder to see what Andy was doing, which game he was play-ing, wondering if he was winning.

"I'd say the answer is yes," she said.

"The food is probably terrible," he warned.

"I don't think he'll notice," she said.

"What about us?" he asked.

She looked startled and he realized she'd misunderstood the what about us remark. When she figured out he was talking about the food, she recovered quickly.

"It can't be as bad as the frozen stuff your foster mother served, can it?" she asked lightly.

"You remembered that?" he asked, taking a drink of his draft beer.

"You just told me last night."

"Last night," he said. "It seems like a lifetime ago."

"What's going to become of him?" she asked, her eyebrows drawn together.

He shook his head. What could he say that he hadn't already said before? He took a deep breath. "He's going back to the orphanage."

"What about the flu epidemic?"

"If he's had a flu shot, it shouldn't matter," he said.

"Shouldn't matter? Shouldn't matter if he's shut up in an orphanage where the flu is rife? How will he sleep if the other kids are up coughing and sneezing all night?"

"Not everyone is sick. The kids with the flu will be in the infirmary." The infirmary. The memories came rushing back. The flu, the measles, the mumps. You name it, he'd had it. "Look, Claire, I'm trying to find him a foster home. I'm doing my best. I've got my admin working on it and she's very good."

"Will she have one by Monday?" she asked.

"She's not that good," he admitted.

"Then what...?"

"I don't know what will happen," he said, his jaw clenched. "I suggest we take this one day at a time. If you have any other ideas, I'd like to hear them."

"I'll take him," she said.

"You'll what?"

"Do foster parents have to be married?" she asked, propping her elbows on the narrow table and leaning forward.

"You're the second person who's asked me that this weekend. I think you can guess who the first one was. The answer is, I don't know. Before you do anything rash, I suggest you think this over. Being a foster parent is a huge responsibility."

"Which you would know," she said, her eyes narrowed.

"I would know better than most."

"I'm just asking, that's all. Don't you agree that I'd at least be better than the family they've lined up for him?" she asked.

"Definitely. Anyone would be better than them. Even me," he said.

"Are you thinking…?"

"…of becoming a foster parent? Not me. I'd be the worst. Well, not the worst, but as you see, I'd never be around. Just the kind of dad no kid should have."

"But here you are spending the weekend with a child. And I thought you said everything went smoothly at the office without you. So why…?"

"This weekend is an aberration," he said flatly. "Monday morning I'll be back at work. A big meeting, a big contract at stake with a company we've been courting for a long time."

"But aren't you enjoying some time off? I could have sworn you got a kick out of flying the kite and building the castle and even playing those video games. Or are you just pretending for Andy's sake?"

He shook his head. "I don't pretend," he said flatly.

"Making up for a childhood you never had?" she suggested gently.

He set his beer glass down with a thud. She was coming a little too close for comfort. He didn't know the answers to her questions and he wasn't in the mood to dig down and find out.

"I don't need any pop psychology to find out if I'm having a good time and if so, why," he said. "I don't want to be analyzed either, so can we talk about something else? Let's talk about you and try to figure out why you want to take on the responsibility of a child who isn't yours, when you specifically told me you didn't need a husband or child to be fulfilled. Not with your satisfying career that lets you take care of yourself. Wasn't that what you said?" he asked.

"I was talking about marriage," she said, squaring her shoulders. "I don't need a husband. I don't need a child either, but since this one appeared on my doorstep, so to speak, I can't turn my back on him—the way you can."

"Me? Turn my back on him? Look, I'm spending my weekend with him. I have my office staff working on his case. What more do you want me to do?"

"Nothing," she said, dropping her gaze and taking a sip of her soda. "I'm sorry. I don't know what got into me." She brushed her hand across her eyes. "I shouldn't have said that. You've done more than anyone could expect from you. I'm worried about him, and I got carried away. You're right, I shouldn't even consider being a foster parent. Or any kind of parent. I love kids, but not twenty-four hours a day. No, I'm a career woman with enough on my plate. We'll take it one day at a time. Maybe tomorrow a miracle will happen."

"Yeah, right. A miracle. In case it doesn't, we ought to do something with him. Before he goes back. Maybe he'd like to go to the zoo or Golden Gate Park."

"I wish I'd brought my bike," she said wistfully. "They close off the roads in the park for bikes on Sundays."

"You can rent one," he said.

"Could I? I wonder if Andy…?"

"We'll ask him," he said.

"What about you?" she asked. "If you don't ride, maybe you'd rather go to the zoo. Or if you have something else to do, say with your girlfriend…"

"I have nothing else to do, and I have no girlfriend. Is that clear? And I know how to ride a bicycle."

At that moment the pizza arrived and so did Andy. He was wearing a hat made of balloons and in between bites of pizza he breathlessly described every game he'd played and won.

Nate glanced at Claire across the table. Her face was positively glowing as she listened to the kid. She met Nate's gaze for a moment, and he realized he was sharing something special with her, something he'd never shared with anyone, a nebulous something he didn't know what to call or how to identify. Was it pride? Was it joy?

Was it true he was only enjoying this because he was making up for the childhood he'd never had? Was he vicariously living another childhood through the boy? Of course not. She didn't know what she was talking about. In any case, he found it hard to tear his gaze away from hers. He didn't want the feeling to go away. He wanted to prolong the moment.

The boy's happy chatter, the look in Claire's eyes

and the warm feeling around his heart made his chest feel like it might burst. All from sharing a pizza with an orphan and a librarian he'd never seen before yesterday and after tomorrow wouldn't be likely to see again. Was he crazy? Was he suffering from sunstroke? True, his face felt slightly burned. But that didn't explain how he felt tonight.

The cynic in him said that warm feeling was just the result of the cheese, tomato sauce and sausage on the pizza. No, it wasn't the greatest meal he'd ever had. In fact, just considering the food, it was one of the worst. But when they left the restaurant, Andy loaded down with cheap trinkets, balloons on his head and a grin on his face, Nate couldn't remember having had a better time at a dinner anywhere. Andy grabbed his hand on the way to the car and Nate felt a lump in his throat. Again he told himself it was probably the indigestible pizza.

When broached about Sunday's activities, Andy looked apprehensive. He said he didn't know how to ride a bike. Nate confessed he hadn't ridden one since he was a teen. He didn't tell either of them that he'd "borrowed" a bike at school because he didn't have one of his own, and wobbled down the street before he caught on. He rode about a mile before he turned around and headed back, faster and faster, thinking every minute that someone was after him. Either the owner or the cops. That was one time he lucked out. He brought it back and no one ever knew.

No one had taught him to ride a bike. No one had taught him anything. He'd learned everything he knew on his own, from watching and listening and doing and from reading. Along the way he'd often thought there were easier ways, but none, perhaps, more effective. Is that how he'd bring up a child of his? No way. He'd teach him everything he knew. Make life easier than he'd had it. A lot easier. He wouldn't wish his childhood on anyone.

Claire was nervous about the sleeping arrangements. She didn't want to ask Nate. Before anyone said anything about sleeping, she volunteered to sleep on the sofa. It was only right. It was her turn.

"No," he said firmly, standing in the middle of the high-ceilinged open area. "Here's how it goes. Andy gets the loft." He nodded to the ladder which led to the low-ceilinged, A-framed storage space above them. "It's just his size, and, in fact, he's already got it." Sure enough, the boy was happily ensconced in a sleeping bag Nate had put there for him. Andy leaned over and grinned down at them, obviously thrilled with his own secret hideaway.

"You get my room," Nate continued, "and I have the sofa. It folds out. It's really quite comfortable, they tell me."

Claire wondered who'd told him. Who had spent the night here? If it was a woman, didn't she spend the night in bed with him? Wasn't that the life of a playboy, after all?

"All the more reason," she said, "for me to sleep there. After all, I made you sleep on the sofa at my house, and it didn't even fold out. It must have been dreadfully uncomfortable. I don't know how you got any sleep."

"I didn't. Does that mean I want to subject you to the same? I have a lot of faults, but I'm not vindictive," he said.

"I didn't think so," she murmured.

"Besides, I've spent worse nights. Doubled up in my car on surveillance, for example. Drinking a gallon of coffee. Trying to stay awake. Your couch was a definite upgrade from those days."

She wanted to protest, to insist that she take the couch, but she sensed that it wouldn't do any good. The look on his face told her the matter was settled.

"I take it you don't have to do that kind of thing anymore," she said.

"We hire young, eager twenty-somethings who are just starting out in the business," he said. "They don't mind the irregular hours, the discomfort. They're just happy to be in such a glamorous, exciting field. They're eager and ambitious, like I was. On the other hand, I find myself spending too much time in the office, sitting at a desk. That wasn't why I went into detective work. I realized today what I've been missing."

"What's that? A day off?" she asked.

"More than that. I'm missing a life. I've been on a treadmill for so long I didn't know what else I could or should be doing."

"You mean you never take a day off?" she asked.

"Do you?" he asked. "You asked me at dinner if I enjoyed playing all day at the beach. I didn't know what to say. Enjoyment is not the word I'd use. It was more of an eye-opener. It's taking some time to sink in. Tell me, when was the last time you flew a kite, rode a bicycle or just goofed off for a whole day?"

"Well, I…"

"That's what I thought," he said. "Admit it, your idea of a good time is reading a journal about children's literature. You're as bad as I am."

"I go to movies," she said.

"With who?" he asked.

"I don't need company at a movie," she said. How dare he suggest she had no life either, no friends, no one to go out with. She put her hands on her hips. "Look, after two days, you don't really know anything about me. About what I do in my spare time. Unlike you, I do have a life. A house that's a home. And a job which is emotionally satisfying."

He held up his arms in mock surrender. "Whatever you say. You have a life and I don't. Grab your bag and come on into my bedroom, I'll show you where everything is."

"Now?" She wasn't ready to see his bedroom. It was too soon. Too intimate. But how could she tell him that? She'd sound like an idiot.

"Yes, now," he said.

All she could think was that the room was not anything like she'd imagined it. It was way too sophisticated for a rough-and-ready macho P.I. A huge bed made of dark oak. A thick gray comforter strewn with gray and black and white pillows. An armoire of the same beautiful wood as the bed. A stone tile floor and a skylight. Large-paned windows would fill with afternoon light and let the noises of the city waft in— muted car horns, whistles and even a whiff of the waters of the bay.

Her quick glance at his bedside table took in a history book and a biography. She had gathered he was self-educated. Now she knew how. The whole effect of this urban sophistication, this display of expensive good taste was to nibble away at the picture she had formed of him and his life. She wasn't ready to make any major alterations to that picture. Not yet. It required too much of an effort. And she was getting tired.

"This is too…" she began. "I can't stay here."

"What's wrong with it?" he asked, frowning. "Too cold? Close the window. Turn the heat up if you want. Make yourself at home."

At home? Make herself at home in this very masculine lair? With the faint scent of shaving lotion in the air? How would she do that? "Thank you. The thing is…this place…it's yours," she said weakly.

"Of course it's mine. Your house was yours. But I slept there. I didn't complain. Except about the couch. Now I'm going to make some coffee to wash down that horrible pizza," he said.

"I didn't think it was that bad," she said, her arguments deflated. She followed him to the kitchen. If that's what she was supposed to do. Or was she supposed to stay in the bedroom he'd assigned her and quit bothering him? She had no idea what was expected of an overnight guest. She'd had only two in the past ten years. And both were last night. For all she knew she'd violated all the rules in the book by inviting a single, unattached man and a runaway orphan to share her house. But these were unusual times. Nate was an unusual man. Unusual in admitting that his life was lacking. That was something *she* wasn't prepared to do. Not to him anyway.

He seemed not to mind her being there, sitting awkwardly on a stool at the breakfast bar. But she knew she was only in this loft because he needed a baby-sitter. And if he intended all of them to go to the park tomorrow together, then she wasn't needed at all.

"About tomorrow…" she said, watching him scoop coffee from a stainless steel container.

He turned to look at her, measuring coffee with one hand, measuring her with his gaze. "Don't tell me you're going to chicken out?" he said.

"I was going to say that you brought me along as a baby-sitter and now that you don't need one maybe I should go home."

"A baby-sitter. Did I say that?" he asked.

"Yes, you did."

"I'm sorry. I didn't mean it that way. I thought you were having a good time. But if you're not, don't let me keep you here against your will. Let me remind you that you're the one who suggested bike-riding. You're the one who said it's good exercise and whatever other benefits you mentioned."

"Non-pollutant and saves on fuel," she reminded him.

"Well?"

"Well, of course I'd like to bike-ride in the park. But what is the purpose if you're coming along?"

"Would you rather I didn't?" he asked.

"Oh, for heaven's sake," she said. No matter what she said he turned it around on her. "No, you should come. Didn't you just say that you knew how to ride a bike, and that today was an eye-opener? That you were missing a life? You did, I heard you." He didn't answer. He just stared at her. Now was her chance to make her exit. "Now that that's settled, I'll go off to bed."

He looked at his watch. "No, you won't. I kept you up last night, talking, telling you the story of my life. Now it's your turn. Sit down." He pointed to a chair in the corner and handed her a cup of coffee with creamer in it. She wondered how he remembered how she took her coffee. Or was it just a lucky guess? She sat down in the surprisingly comfortable chair she vaguely recognized from a well-known furniture designer and looked at him. Now he was on a stool, coffee in front of him, his elbows on the breakfast bar, looking like he was waiting for her to begin. But there was no way she was going to share with him or anyone the details of her life.

"Look," she said. "The story of my life is not that interesting. Not like yours. I was an army brat. Moved around a lot. Loved to read. Became a librarian. End of story."

"Where did you move to?"

She ticked off the cities and the states, hoping he'd get bored and they could move on to another subject. Any subject but her life. But he didn't. He asked more questions and reluctantly she answered. Until he asked about her parents. She took a deep breath, determined to resist. Determined to put an end to the evening and go to bed. She couldn't imagine anyone that interested in her life story. No one ever had been before. But for some reason he was. And for some reason she couldn't resist. Couldn't resist the way he was looking at her, listening to her as if she was the most fascinating person he'd ever met. If she was, the others must have been real duds. So instead of telling him how tired she was, instead of making an excuse, pleading a headache and going to bed, she continued.

"My mother died when I was young, as you know. My father was a typical army officer. Tough, disciplined and uncompromising. He wanted a boy and he got me. I don't think he ever got over the disappointment. He certainly never banked on having to raise a girl by himself. So he didn't. I pretty much raised myself. That's why..."

She broke off. Before she knew it she was going to have blabbed her whole life story. Against her will. Surely Nate hadn't counted on that when he started this conversation. If you could call a monologue a conversation.

"That's why you don't know if you could raise a child," he suggested.

She sucked in a sharp breath. How did he know that? "I guess so," she admitted. "It's a scary proposition. But we're not talking about just any child. We're talking about Andy."

"Are you serious? You certainly wouldn't consider taking him on by yourself, would you?"

She shook her head. "I don't know. I don't think I could or that I should. All I know is that I can't bear to return him to the orphanage, and I certainly don't want to send him to a foster home, not the kind you've told me about. But you're right. I don't know how to raise a child. Do you?"

"Of course not," he said. "Raising a child is the furthest thing from my mind. Which is not to say that I won't do everything I can to find the kid a good home. I will. In the meantime, we were talking about you."

"There's nothing more to tell, really."

"You never told me why you wanted to run away."

"Oh, that."

"Yes, that. Come on, I spilled my guts to you the other night and you're holding out on me."

She hesitated a long moment. She could have kicked herself for admitting she had planned to run away. What had gotten into her anyway? What to say? How much to tell him? She'd already told him more than she'd ever told anyone. Why was that? Because

they were the ships that passed in the night and tomorrow or the day after that he'd sail out of her life
forever? Or was it the fact that he'd had an unhappy
childhood too?

"It was a long time ago," she said, hoping to stall
for time.

"I'm glad to hear it," he said as his mouth quirked
in a wry smile. "There's something disturbing about
a grown woman running away from home."

"Laugh if you want," she said, giving him a self-
righteous look. "But you asked me and I'm trying to
explain."

"Sorry," he said, getting off the stool to refill her
coffee cup. When his hand brushed hers as he took
the cup she felt a shiver go up her spine. Without
saying anything, he set the cup down, took off his
sweater and draped it over her shoulders. She opened
her mouth to protest, to say she wasn't cold, but then
she'd have to admit she was shivering because he
made her nervous, made her feel like a different person than the woman he'd met two days ago, who spent
her days at the library and her evenings at home reading.

In the space of two days she had become exquisitely
sensitive to cool breezes and hot sun and his touch.
Especially his touch on her skin. Her skin was full of
nerve endings she didn't know existed. His sweater
was warm and transferred his body heat to her. She
could feel it seep into her body. She could smell his
masculine scent surrounding her and she forgot what
they were talking about, what she'd been about to say.

"Better?" he asked with his hands on her shoulders.

Afraid to trust her voice, she merely nodded. She
didn't want him to move. She wanted him to stay

where he was, with his sweater around her shoulders and his hands kneading slightly, sending waves of pleasure to the core of her body. But he didn't, he took his hands away, crossed the room and went back to his perch on the stool.

"You were going to tell me why you wanted to run away. When you were a child, that is."

"Yes, well, after my mother died when I was eleven, my father retreated into his job. Not that he'd ever been what you'd call a family man, but then he barely noticed I existed. We'd never had a close relationship, but somehow I thought he'd come around and start being a dad, and he didn't. As he retreated into his job, spent his evenings at the officers' club, I retreated into books, into a make-believe world where kids had big, happy families. Where they did things together, like go to the beach or the zoo or the circus. I always wanted to go to the circus. My father said it was childish. He said I was too old for that nonsense. I probably was. Anyway, that was the end of that."

"What about bike-riding in the park?" he asked. "Was that something else you never got to do?"

She nodded. "I see what you're getting at. You think I'm consciously or unconsciously trying to make up for my lost childhood by taking Andy under my wing and experiencing all the things I never got to do."

"I didn't say that," he said. "Knowing you, it could be a purely altruistic gesture. Or some of both."

"Knowing me? You don't know me. How could you know me?" Yet even as she said the words, she realized he already knew her better than anyone she'd worked with, anyone she'd gone to school with or lived next door to. But she wasn't quite sure how and when it had happened.

"How could I?" he asked. "Let's see. Since I met you, I've spent a night under your roof, eaten your pot roast and shared a pizza with you. As for you, you've fainted at my feet, you've taken an orphan under your wing, cooked dinner for the orphan and a man you didn't know, built a sand castle, bared your soul—and part of your body...."

She knew from the wicked gleam in his eye he was teasing her, which caused the color to rush to her face once again. "That suit," she said. "I should never have worn it. It's too...too tight, too revealing."

"It was? I didn't notice," he said blandly.

She didn't believe him. He was teasing her again. He'd already made note of that suit. Yes, it would be a relief to know she hadn't made a spectacle of herself. On the other hand, if he was really serious, she'd feel more than a trace of disappointment. If he hadn't noticed, why hadn't he? Was she that uninteresting? Did she just blend in with the other oversized bodies stuffed into skintight swimsuits on the beach, while he stood out like the good-looking, well-muscled man he was?

One thing she knew, her eyes had been glued to him while he slept as well as when he ran down the beach. And she wasn't the only one who'd noticed him. She'd seen more than a few females turn their heads in his direction, which wasn't at all surprising. What was surprising was that no one had talked him into marriage yet. Was he really too busy? Was he really that set against it, afraid to take a chance, as afraid as she was that he couldn't make it work?

"Back to your running away," he prompted, refilling his own coffee cup from the pot on the counter.

"I never ran away," she protested. "The only reason I even thought about it was that I missed my mother. I don't know where I would have run to. We moved around so often I had no place that seemed like home. No place and nobody to run to. Actually, an army base is a very secure place, as I told Andy in the car. Everything you need is there. Everyone knows everyone, so there was no reason to run away."

"None at all?" he asked. He studied her face for such a long time she had to look away. She had the feeling he could see inside her. That he knew about the terrible incident in high school without her even mentioning it, the time she'd come the closest to really running away. And that he wasn't going to give up until she'd told him about it.

She thought about excusing herself and going to bed. She could easily plead fatigue. After all, she hadn't napped on the beach the way he had. She should be tired, but she felt wide-awake, as if she'd been wired. Maybe it was the coffee, she thought, staring into her half-empty cup. And maybe it wasn't. Maybe it was the fact that a man had stepped out of the pages of a detective novel and entered her life in a way she'd never expected. And very soon he'd leave the same way he'd arrived, and return full-time to his life here in the city. To his job and his philanthropy and his so-called girlfriend. But while he was here, while they shared a common interest in the orphan boy, she wanted to stay awake and alert. There'd be plenty of time to sleep after this extraordinary episode was over.

So if she didn't retreat to bed, she could simply

refuse to answer his question or change the subject. But then he'd know she was hiding something and it would make him more tenacious than ever. Why was he being so tenacious? Why did he care? She couldn't understand it. But there it was. And he didn't seem likely to give up until she'd come clean. What did it matter anyway? It was a long time ago and it had nothing to do with anything.

"No reason to run away at all," she said. "The last time I ever seriously contemplated running away from home was because of a small incident that in retrospect wasn't the least bit important."

"Then you won't mind telling me about it," he said.

"I promise you won't find it interesting. You'll think I was crazy to get so upset."

"Why don't you let me decide?"

She shrugged, trying for a nonchalant look before she blurted out the brief, shameful story. Then she fixed her gaze on a clock on the wall behind the counter where Nate sat and took a deep breath.

"Okay, there were these guys in my class in high school. Football players, very macho, very popular. I didn't pay any attention to them. They were out of my orbit. My orbit being the school newspaper and the library where I had a part-time job. But I knew who they were. You'd have to be blind not to notice them. I never dreamed they'd noticed me. At most I figured I was just a fly on the wall to them. But one day they came into the library just before closing." She'd started out speaking so calmly, but suddenly it all came back to her in a rush and her voice faltered. The fear, the shame, and the embarrassment almost overwhelmed her. Her throat threatened to close up on her.

It felt like sandpaper. She picked up her coffee cup, but her hand was shaking so much she couldn't get it to her mouth.

Nate jumped to his feet. "Claire," he said alarmed. "Are you all right? You're pale. You're not going to faint on me again, are you?"

"Of course not." She set her cup down with a clatter. "I'm fine. Where was I?"

"High school. In the library. But if this is too painful for you…?" He stood with his arms braced against the counter, looking concerned.

"No, no. Not at all," she said, determined to finish the story once and for all and then, by heaven, she'd never speak of it again. "It doesn't bother me a bit," she insisted. "I was in the library and they came in all at once, two or three of them, I don't remember." But she did remember. She remembered as if it was yesterday. "There were three of them wearing varsity-letter jackets. They didn't just walk in, they swaggered. They asked for books about sex. They picked up books and tossed them on the floor. They laughed at me, made fun of my glasses, my baggy clothes. Then one of them pushed me up against the bookshelf and held me there with his hands on my shoulders…" She got up and crossed the room, put her hands on Nate's shoulders.

"Like this," she said, pushing him back against the counter. "And he touched me here…and there…." She put her hands on his chest.

She didn't know she was crying until Nate's face blurred in front of her. He wrapped his arms around her and held her tight. For some reason this gesture, meant to calm her and comfort her, made her cry even harder. Great gulping sobs she couldn't control. He murmured comforting words and massaged her shoulders, running his hands down her back and stroking her hips.

"It's okay. They're gone. They won't be back," he said.

"I know, I know," she sobbed. "Mrs. Monroe came in. The librarian. They ran away."

"But they didn't hurt you, did they?" he asked, wiping the tears from her cheeks with his fingers.

"No," she said, catching her breath. "That's why it's so stupid for me to get so upset. I wasn't hurt. But...but..."

"But it did hurt. It hurt deep inside," he said knowingly. He pulled her so close her tear-streaked face was pressed against his shirt, and she could hear his heartbeat, strong and steady, and smell the fresh scent of his clean shirt. She wanted to stay there forever, locked in his arms. Warm, safe and protected. She knew she should pull away. She knew this was not a forever moment. Nate Callahan was not a forever kind of man. He was just being kind. Just being sympathetic.

She told herself to go back and sit down, or better yet, call it an evening and escape into his tailored, masculine room. But her knees were weak and her will was even weaker. Her shoes were made of lead and she couldn't move. Instead, she sagged against him, letting him support her. Letting him kiss the last trace of tears from her cheeks.

The atmosphere suddenly changed. She didn't know how, she didn't know why. It was as if there'd been a rise in the atmospheric pressure. It was so thick and so real she could almost touch it, almost feel it around her. All at once his kisses turned passionate. He cradled her face in his hands and he kissed her on the lips. Hard and fast and furious. She knew then this had nothing to do with sympathy, nothing to do with kindness. She no longer needed either. She needed something else. Something more.

His mouth covered hers with rough insistence. Devouring her, taking her breath away, taking her innocence, demanding her surrender. But she didn't surrender. She met his kisses with her own. How she'd learned how to kiss like that she had no idea. Maybe she'd seen it in a movie. Maybe she'd read about it. Maybe it came out of some deep desire she'd buried long ago. Maybe it came out of her soul.

His body was rock hard against her. His mouth was wet and hungry. The most incredible sensations raced through her body. Sensations she'd never read about or seen in movies. Sensations that built and built until she thought they had nowhere to go. Until she wanted more. She wanted to get closer to him. Wanted to feel his hands on her body. Wanted him to carry her off somewhere and make love to her. She wanted to know what she'd been missing all these years.

She might have found out if the phone hadn't rung.

He stopped in midkiss as if he'd been stung by a deadly wasp. She rocked backward on her heels. Her head was spinning.

"Damn, damn, damn," he muttered.

Chapter Seven

He didn't *have* to answer it, she thought as she stumbled blindly toward his bedroom. If it had been her phone, her house, and she'd been kissing him the way he'd kissed her, she would have let it ring. Oh, yes, it would have taken more than a phone call to pull her out of his arms. An earthquake might have done it. Say a 7.9 or so on the Richter scale. Or a firestorm. Or maybe a major hurricane would have done it.

But for Nate, all it took was a phone call. That's how little the kiss meant to him. Judging from the way he lunged for the receiver just as she skittered out of the room. She didn't want to hear a word of his conversation. It was none of her business who would be calling him at this hour of the night. She had no business eavesdropping. But she couldn't deny she was curious. So curious she stood in the doorway of the bedroom shamelessly listening.

"Diana," he said. "I got your message.... Sorry

about that. I was working.... I've told you over and over not to count on me. Things come up.''

There was a long silence. Diana must be some long-winded woman, Claire thought.

"No one you know," he said. "Just a friend.... No, not a girlfriend. A friend. It's late. I'll call you tomorrow.... Yes, she's here. We're working on a project together. It's business. I don't care if you believe me or not. It's the truth. You knew from the beginning I wasn't interested in a long-term relationship.... Never have been. Never will be. Goodbye.''

He said goodbye, but she didn't hear him hang up. Maybe he did, or maybe she was still talking and he was still listening. Claire took the opportunity to close the bedroom door, shimmy out of her clothes and into the flannel nightgown she'd brought. She'd just dived into his king-sized bed and pulled the comforter up to her chin when he knocked on the door.

"Yes?'' her voice came out like a squeak. She was amazed it came out at all.

He came into the room and closed the door behind him. She wondered if it was too late to pretend to be asleep.

"Sorry about that,'' he said.

She didn't know what he was sorry about, kissing her or answering the phone.

"It happens,'' she said, trying to sound nonchalant, when under the covers her knees were knocking together so loudly she was afraid he could hear them. *It happens* could refer to the kiss or the phone call. It was an all-purpose answer and she was proud of herself for thinking of it.

"It might happen to you,'' he said, leaning against

the door. "But it doesn't happen to me. Not that often."

She took a deep breath. "If you're talking about getting a phone call in the middle of the night…"

"I'm not talking about the phone call. I should never have answered it. I thought it might be important. It wasn't," he said flatly. "I'm talking about what happened before the phone call."

"Oh, that," she said, trying to dismiss it as if it was nothing. "It was my fault. I don't know what got into me. I don't usually go around crying on people's shoulders."

"Is that what I am? People?" he asked, glaring at her.

"No, of course not," she assured him. "I don't know why I said that. I appreciate your…your sympathy."

"Sympathy had nothing to do with it," he said harshly. "You don't understand, do you? I couldn't keep my hands off you. And it was not because I felt sorry for you. You're right about one thing. It *was* your fault. Your fault for looking so damned sexy in that huge shirt of yours. Making me want to see what's underneath. Making me want to rip it off you."

It was a good thing she was lying in bed because if she'd been standing, she'd have fallen over with surprise. Sexy? Rip it off her? Had he taken leave of his senses? Was he crazy?

"Me?" she said. "Sexy?"

"You," he said, pointing his finger at her. "You don't know it, but you have the sexiest body I've ever seen. All the more so because you don't know it and because you cover it up. I admit it. I'm accustomed to women who flaunt their bodies. Who come on strong. You're different.''

She sat up straight, her back stiffened against the headboard, letting the comforter fall to her lap. ''You don't have to tell me how different I am. I've known that since puberty when I got glasses, grew five inches and went from a training bra to a 36D. All in the space of a year. Seventh grade. Oh, I was different all right. And I didn't know how to handle it except by wearing big, shapeless clothes and hiding out after school in the library. My father handled it by ignoring me. My teachers did the same. The boys in my class made remarks and snickered. And then there was that day....'' She sighed. Why go on? He'd already heard more than he wanted to know about her painful adolescence.

''I wish I'd been there. I would have punched them out,'' he said socking one fist into his hand.

She shook her head. ''No, you wouldn't. No seventh-grade boy would stand up for a big, awkward girl in glasses who stumbled over her size-nine feet when a boy looked at her.''

''Sounds like they did more than look the day in the library,'' he said.

''That was only one day. I overreacted, okay? Because I didn't know how to handle it. Just like I did in the kitchen, crying all over your shirt.'' She'd really done a job on his shirt. It still looked wet and crumpled. A reminder of how she'd behaved. Like a love-starved spinster. Which was just what she must seem to him. Which was exactly what she was. That was the sad part. ''I promise I won't let it happen again.''

''Maybe you should,'' he said studying her through narrowed eyes. ''Maybe you should let it happen again. Let go more often. And I'm not just talking about crying.''

"I know what you're talking about. I wish I could explain why I did what I did. I swear I've never..."

"You've never kissed a man you've only known for two days, is that what you were going to say?" he asked.

How could she admit she'd never kissed a man, period? She couldn't let him think that. Or did he know? Could he tell by the way she'd come across, as an overexcited, sexually inexperienced novice? She knew what he was talking about. Those hot kisses they'd exchanged. She hadn't just been on the receiving end. She'd been an active participant. She still didn't understand how she'd even known what to do. How to slant her lips, where to put her hands. It had all happened so fast she wondered if she'd made a complete fool of herself.

"That's right," she said, determined to be as cool as she could, to counteract the image of the spinster librarian. "My rule is never kiss a man you've only known for two days. I always wait at least three days. It works out better that way. Otherwise they get the wrong idea."

"Really? Do they? The idea that you're a loose woman you mean. What about sleeping with them? What's your rule about that?"

"Oh. Well..." She stared at the wall, trying to think. Wishing she'd turned out the light ten minutes ago, before he came into the room, because he was making her nervous standing there, his arms crossed over his chest, leaning against the door frame, his face half in shadow, staring at her and asking questions she couldn't answer.

"Can I get back to you on that?" she asked, trying to sound glib. Trying to sound like someone who routinely kissed men in their kitchen and then spent the night in their bed. But she didn't feel glib, she felt light-headed and dizzy and tongue-tied.

Instead of answering he smiled. A smile that was not the mocking smile she expected. It was a reluctant smile that tugged at his mouth and made her heart race. A sudden warmth spread through her body, making her wish she could toss off the blankets and replace her flannel nightgown with something lighter, like nothing at all.

Instead of answering he asked a question of his own. "Comfortable?" he asked.

"Yes, very. Thank you very much. It doesn't seem fair, my taking your bed. Are you sure you don't want to…?"

"Join you? I thought you'd never ask." He was teasing her as she'd never been teased by a man in her life. It threw her off guard. She didn't know how to respond. How to tease and flirt the way other women did.

Instead, she pursed her lips together in an effort to look stern. "I was going to say, are you sure you don't want to sleep here?"

"Was that an invitation?" he asked.

With that she kicked back the covers, swung her legs to the floor and stood up. It wasn't easy given the way her knees almost buckled under her, but her determination to put an end to this ridiculous byplay overcame her shyness at being seen in her nightgown. After all, hadn't he seen her last night in her nightgown? "That's it. I'm taking the couch," she said. "This is your bed and you belong in it."

He crossed the room in two giant strides. He picked her up and held her against his chest for a long moment, gazing into her eyes while the air whooshed out of her lungs and her heart banged against her ribs. Just like he'd done when she'd fainted. Only then she hadn't been as aware of his smoldering gray-green eyes, of the dark outline of the shadow of a beard along his jaw.

"This is my bed and *you* belong in it," he said. "I thought we settled that hours ago."

"Put me down," she said, with a feeble, ineffectual motion of one hand.

He tightened his grip, pulling her closer until her face was only a breath away.

"Are you sure that's what you want?" he asked, his voice low. His eyes darkened, and she wasn't sure of anything anymore. Her head was spinning with images of him in that bed with her. She wondered what would happen if she did invite him. She knew she was acting irrationally. She had to force herself to be sensible. To get hold of her erotic thoughts. To remember why she was there—not to fall into Nate Callahan's arms, but to take care of one small boy who needed all the attention he could get.

"I'm not sure of anything," she murmured honestly.

So he put her down. Put her down on the cool sheets and sat on the edge of the bed next to her. She didn't know what to say. How can you order a man out of his own bedroom, especially when you really don't want him to go?

"Let me know when you make up your mind," he said. He reached out and touched her flushed cheek, trailing his fingers down to the hollow of her throat where her pulse beat wildly. Then his hands moved down to the soft flowered flannel of her nightgown to the swell of her breasts where he circled her nipples so slowly and so gently she didn't think she could bear the exquisite pleasure.

Waves of white-hot desire almost tore her in two. The fabric between his hands and her skin felt like an obstacle, so much in the way, she wanted to pull the nightgown over her head and toss it on the floor. But she didn't. She closed her eyes and moaned softly.

With her last coherent breath, she knew what she had to do.

"You'd better go," she said.

When she opened her eyes he was gone. She thought she'd be relieved, but she was disappointed. Let down. She didn't know what she'd expected. After all, she'd told him to go. But now that he was gone, the suave, urbane, masculine room that had seemed so perfect seemed cold and lifeless. She turned off the light and snuggled down under the comforter once again. She was exhausted. Her whole body throbbed with unknown and unnamed sensations. The sheets enveloped her in a heady scent that was pure Nate. She buried her face in his pillow and moaned once again. What had she done? She'd made a fool of herself, that's what she'd done.

But his words went round and round in her brain. *Sexiest body I've ever seen. You're different.*

And those other words she'd overheard. *Not interested in a long-term relationship. Never have been. Never will be.*

Claire didn't know what time she finally fell asleep. She could always blame the noises of the city for keeping her awake, but the truth was, it was her wide-awake mind that kept her tossing and turning until dawn. The strange thing was that she didn't wake up until the sun was shining in the window, as bright as if it was at least nine o'clock. She, who never overslept, even on the weekends, had apparently overslept in a strange house in a strange man's bed. She lay there for a long moment, wondering if she'd dreamed the whole evening, the kisses, the tears, the touch of his hands on her body. She stared at the ceiling, thinking she smelled coffee and heard voices.

She tiptoed across the floor and put her ear to the door. Not only voices, but laughter. Masculine laughter. She knew it was late, but before she faced anyone she had to have a shower. Maybe then she'd feel more normal. More like the librarian she was a few days ago before this man had walked into her life. She jumped into the shower in the adjoining bathroom with its double sinks, its vanity of slab limestone and its rack of towels. She gasped at the size of the bathroom, at least as big as her bedroom at home.

Even the bathroom had a view of the San Francisco Bay from the window next to the sunken tub. She thought enviously how nice it would be to lie there in hot water gazing out at the freighters gliding out to sea. Did Nate do that? Or was the tub something the decorator put in the way she'd done the kitchen? Was he so busy he only had time for a hasty shower?

Back in the bedroom she pulled a pair of slacks and a sweater from her overnight bag. To her horror, she discovered the sweater she'd packed in a hurry while Nate and Andy had waited for her yesterday, had shrunk in the laundry. She'd meant to have it dry-cleaned, but had washed and dried it instead. Instead of hiding her body the way it was meant to do, it was clinging to her curves. She stood in the middle of Nate's room staring at herself in the mirror above the table. She tugged at the ribbing around her waist and stretched the wool with her fingers. It did no good. The sweater just retracted and went back into place. Everything Nate had said to her about her clothes and her body came back to haunt her.

Women would kill for a body like that...flaunt it, not hide it...you're different.

She knew she was different. She hadn't known she might be different in a good way until Nate came along. Was he right about her body? Was she being overly sensitive by covering it up from head to toe in extra-large-sized clothes? Was it time she grew out of being obsessed about her size? It seemed she had no choice today, unless she pulled her sweatshirt over the sweater to hide her breasts, but given the sun outside, and the warmth of the apartment, it seemed like overkill. She took a deep breath, squared her shoulders and walked into the kitchen and found total chaos.

Flour was all over the floor. Eggshells were scattered on the beautiful granite counter, at least a dozen of them, along with spilled milk and every utensil known to professional and amateur chef alike.

"What happened?" she asked.

Andy who was perched on a stool with his elbows on the counter looked up and giggled. His eyes were beaming and his shirt was covered with flour.

Nate just stared. If she'd thought he wouldn't notice her too-tight sweater she was mistaken. His eyes were riveted on her breasts.

"We're making pancakes," Andy said.

"Right," Nate said, jerking his eyes away and tapping a spoon against a large bowl as if he was trying to jar his wayward attention back to the job at hand. "We've had a few mishaps along the way, but I think we're on our way now. I don't suppose you know how to make pancakes, do you?"

"Well, yes. But don't let me interfere," she said.

"We need some advice, don't we, pal?" he asked the boy.

Andy nodded. "I'm readin' the recipe on the box and Nate does what it says. But there's some parts we don't understand."

"To say the least," Nate said.

"Let me see," Claire said, brushing some flour off Andy's shirt. "Where did you get all these ingredients? I could have sworn the refrigerator and your cupboards were bare last night."

"Last night was last night," Nate said. "Today is another day. I woke up early and so did Andy. I was going out for bagels when he said he'd rather have pancakes. So we hit the mom-and-pop store on the corner. They told us what to buy, but they didn't tell us how to make them. We thought, we hoped, you'd be up when we got back. But you weren't. So we proceeded without you. That may have been a mistake."

"I'm sorry. I never oversleep. I don't know what happened," she said, running her hand through her damp hair. Reminding her she'd forgotten to pin it back, and now it was hanging around her face.

"Big day yesterday," Nate said with a devilish gleam in his eye. "You were beat. We all were. You must have gotten a good night's sleep. Some of us did, some of us didn't. Some of us were all wound up. Too much coffee. Too much excitement. Too much stimulation.'' He gave her a look that made her face turn crimson. She knew exactly what he was referring to. So it wasn't a dream after all.

"If you didn't sleep well," she said primly, "it was because I was in your bed and..."

"You've got that right," he said under his breath.

"I was in your bed," she continued as if he hadn't spoken. It was the only way to deal with his constant teasing. Ignore it. "And you were on the couch. It couldn't have been that comfortable. I told you..."

"My lack of sleep had nothing to do with the couch. It had everything to do with you in my bed." He shot her a look that said volumes, that fortunately little Andy was oblivious to. "In any case I'm glad you got a good night's sleep because you look great. Doesn't she, Andy?"

The boy nodded obediently. "Now can you help us with the pancakes?" he asked.

He stood there looking at her so patiently, so hopefully, so eagerly, she plunged into the work, giving them each a task—beating eggs, heating syrup, mixing flour while she cleaned up the mess on the floor and the counters. Then she had Andy mix it all up with a big spoon, had Nate set the table and finally they sat down together at the breakfast bar and ate pancakes together like many other families on a Sunday morning. Anyone who was looking in from the skylight above the kitchen might have mistaken them for such a family.

Only they weren't a family. They were one confirmed—*not interested in a long-term relationship*—bachelor, one confirmed spinster who'd never even had a boyfriend let alone come close to marriage and one orphan who was unadoptable because of his advanced age of eight, and was on his way back to the orphanage. All the more reason to make the best of it, she thought. To make it a day to remember for Andy. Not for her. She didn't need any days to remember. She had her own life.

Not for Nate either. He didn't need any day to remember. He had a busy, productive life. Although he did say that yesterday had been an eye-opener. That he'd been on a treadmill. But he never said he wanted to get off the treadmill. She just wanted to believe that he did. Wanted to believe he'd enjoyed it as much as she had. That he wanted to change his life as she'd changed her appearance. That spending a day like that had been good for him. She was sure it had been.

"Are there any more?" Andy asked as he cleaned his plate, scooping up the last drops of syrup with his spoon.

Before Claire could get up, Nate went to the stove, where he tossed the last pancake in the air several times before he flipped it onto Andy's plate. Andy clapped delightedly and Claire watched the interplay between them with a lump in her throat. Every boy should have a dad. A dad to make pancakes with in the morning. The kind of dad she'd never had. She realized that she'd never seen a man in the kitchen trying to cook something. According to Nate, it wasn't anything he ever did either. But here he was. Instead of taking the easy way out and buying bagels, he'd given cooking a try. Claire admired him for that.

"Are we still bike-riding?" she asked Nate when Andy had finished his pancake, drained his milk glass and gone to brush his teeth.

"Of course," he said. "You can't let a kid down. Are you ready?" He cocked his head and allowed his gaze to take in her slacks and then linger on her sweater and the swell of her breasts. She'd almost forgotten about the tight sweater. She wanted to explain what had happened, that she hadn't changed her style, but if she did, she'd just be calling more attention to it. Instead, she stacked the breakfast dishes and hurriedly carried them to the sink.

"What are you doing? Leave everything there. The cleaning woman comes tomorrow," he said.

"Leave everything like this? I can't do that. I thought the rule was the person who doesn't cook does the dishes. That's me. I didn't cook, you did. It serves me right for oversleeping. It will just take a few minutes."

He shrugged. "If you insist. Did I tell you you look great today?" he asked, coming up behind her and breathing into her ear. "There's something different about you. You should oversleep more often."

"What and lose my job? I don't think so." She kept her back to him as she stacked the dishes into the dishwasher. But she knew he was only inches away and it made her knees weak. When she felt his hands on her shoulders, she couldn't ignore him any longer. Especially when he gently turned her around to face him and forced her to look him in the eye.

"Look at you," he said. "Your hair is down, your glasses are gone and your sweater actually fits you. You look beautiful."

She gazed into his green eyes, more gray today under the skylight, and saw that he was sincere. He meant every word he said. He thought she was beautiful. How could that be? No one had ever told her that before. He made her feel as if she was a beautiful, sexy woman and he was a rugged, handsome, sexy man who admired her. She was right about one thing, he was rugged, handsome and sexy. Maybe he did admire her in some way. At his worst he merely loved to tease her, and at his best he really wanted to make her feel better about herself. Which he did. At this moment, she didn't doubt his intentions. There was nothing but genuine admiration in his eyes. And she appreciated that. But Lord help her, she wanted more.

Because deep down, didn't Nate really just admire her for following his advice? Wasn't this some kind of *My Fair Lady* theme, where the hero transforms the guttersnipe into a countess and takes pleasure in seeing her change her image because it makes him feel clever and right? Only in her case, the macho private eye transforms the old-maid librarian into a new woman—at least on the outside. On the inside it wasn't so easy. Deep down, despite what the mirror and the man told her, she was still the five-foot-nine-inch seventh-grader who grew up too fast, who was bigger than all the other girls and was the subject of ridicule.

The silence grew between them while she tried to think of something to say. Some way to brush off the compliment.

"You have a hard time accepting compliments, don't you?" he asked as if he'd read her mind.

"I...I guess I do. That kind anyway. Now if you'd told me I ran a great children's reading program, I think I could accept that."

He tilted her chin with his thumb. "You already know that. You don't know how you look today. So it's my job to tell you."

"I don't know what to say," she said, dropping her gaze to the floor. "Except thank you."

"That's a start," he said.

When he left the kitchen to get his sweater she finished loading the dishwasher.

"Claire," Nate called from the living room. "Let's go. We're waiting for you."

She glanced at her reflection in the door of the microwave oven before she joined them. Yes, she *did* look different. Her face was flushed and her hair framed her face in a way she'd previously thought too messy for a librarian. Then there was the sweater. Much too tight for a librarian. She reminded herself she was off duty today.

Her normal inclination, on any day, would have been to hunch her shoulders so no one would notice her breasts. But today she didn't. She didn't know why, but she deliberately squared her shoulders so her breasts were higher and rounder than ever. She stared at herself for one last moment before Andy called to her, that they were ready.

"I'm coming," she called.

At the bike shop on Stanyan Street next to Golden Gate Park, they rented three bikes in three different sizes. A big one for Nate, a middle-sized bike for Claire and a small one for Andy. Just like the three bears. Claire and Nate chained their bikes to a small tree and spent the first hour teaching Andy to ride by pushing him down a path behind the bandshell. He weaved, he leaned and he almost fell off. But he didn't give up. Claire loved that about him. They guided him from the rear, one hand on the back of his seat, one hand on his handlebars. And they shouted to him.

"Keep pedaling."

"Watch out for other people."

"Don't be afraid. You won't fall."

"I've got you. There you go."

When he finally got his balance and took off without their help they looked at each other and smiled broadly.

"He did it," Nate said.

"I knew he could," Claire said. Her heart swelled with pride.

Nate gave her a quick hug. Right in the middle of the path with people coming and going. It was over before she knew what to do. How to respond. She looked away before he thought that she thought it meant something more than a shared moment of pride in a boy they both cared about. She didn't dare say *loved*. Because if she loved Andy she couldn't bear to let him go, could she?

If they were proud of Andy, he was even prouder of himself. With his head held high and a grin on his face he rode the bike paths round and round the park with Nate and Claire following closely. He wobbled occasionally, but he got steadier and steadier. Claire couldn't help beaming at him and occasionally exchanging glances with Nate who smiled back.

Claire hadn't ridden her bike for pure pleasure for months, maybe years. It was her transportation to and from work, which made her feel good for conserving energy, as she'd told Nate, and getting exercise, but today was a different story. A cool breeze blew, lifting her hair off the back of her neck and the sun warmed her face. She felt like a different person from the one who wore baggy clothes and who'd closed her library on Friday evening to bicycle home with Nate following in his car.

It could be the sweater. Wearing a sweater that fitted her body made her feel different. Sleek, even slender. More feminine, more womanly. Of course part of that new feeling could be attributed to the man who rode alongside. She caught him looking at her with something like approval mixed with something else. Of course he would approve, since she'd taken his advice, so he thought, and worn something that clung to her body. He didn't know that she hadn't done it on purpose, that it was a mistake. Or was it? Had she deliberately put that sweater in her overnight bag, knowing there was the possibility it had shrunk? If she had, it had been her subconscious at work.

They stopped at the bandshell to listen to an orchestra play a selection of traditional songs, but Andy was too restless to sit still for long. He wanted to get back on his bike. So off they went again. Past Stowe Lake with its canoes and toy boats and the glassed-in Victorian arboretum. A while later they persuaded Andy to stop at the Japanese Tea Garden where they sat down in the teahouse for tea and fortune cookies.

"What does yours say?" Nate asked the boy.

Andy handed it to Nate to read. "You will find health and happiness," Nate read.

"What's yours?" Claire asked Nate.

"It says my dream will come true," he said. His voice was laced with skepticism. Claire guessed that even if he had a dream, he wouldn't admit it.

"What's your dream?" Andy asked.

"No dreams," he said. "Dreams are for kids."

"No, they're not," Claire told Andy. "You're never too old to dream."

"What does yours say?" Andy asked Claire.

"My career will take an unusual turn," she said, holding up the tiny scrap of paper. "Maybe I'm going to get my bookmobile at last. Maybe I'll be driving around to the neighborhoods where there are no libraries, getting people hooked on books.''

''You'd like that, wouldn't you?'' Nate asked, studying her from across the small table.

''I think so. Although I'd miss my story hour. What about you? Maybe you had a dream about your job. Maybe it's going to take an unusual turn too.''

''It couldn't happen,'' Nate said flatly. ''I'm stuck with my job and it's my own fault. I've elevated myself to the top of the agency. To make matters worse my partner has decided to spend more time at home in hopes of saving his marriage, which puts more responsibility for running the office on me. I realized over these past few days how much I've missed getting out in the field. How rusty my skills are. You're the one who found Andy here. Not me.''

He ruffled Andy's hair and the boy glanced up at Nate with a shy look in his eyes that made Claire's heart turn over. It told her how much Andy had bonded with the private investigator. How much he needed a man in his life. She sighed. If she'd ever thought she could take Andy in, she knew at that moment it would be wrong. If he had a choice of a two-parent home and her home, she'd have to let him go. Not that she had a choice.

He wasn't hers to let go or to keep. If anyone kept him, it should be Nate. But that didn't look like much of a possibility. Not with Nate's determination to avoid any kind of a family life. She wondered for the hundredth time how they were going to find Andy a good home. Nate had said his office was working on it, but how could someone like his assistant, who didn't know the boy, find the right family for him? Andy didn't seem worried about it, didn't talk about running away anymore, or maybe he was just afraid to ask, afraid to think of the future. Who could blame the boy? She knew how that was. She was afraid to ask too. Afraid to contemplate his future. So many questions, so few answers. She opened another fortune cookie and gasped at the message.

Chapter Eight

"**W**hat is it?" Nate asked, noting her reaction.

She tore the piece of paper into tiny bits. "Nothing," she said. But it was something. The message inside the cookie read: Your secret wish will come true.

Now that didn't make sense. How could her secret wish for love come true if she wouldn't even recognize love if she found it? Did she know what love felt like? All her life she'd longed for it, but never had it. Was it really within her reach? No, that was just wishful thinking, fortune-cookie nonsense.

"Time to go, isn't it?" she asked, setting her teacup down on the table. Andy hadn't drunk his. That wasn't unusual. Not many kids his age liked tea. But he didn't eat his cookies either. Now that *was* unusual. He'd said he wasn't hungry. Maybe it was all those pancakes at breakfast. He put his head on the table, and Claire shot Nate a worried look.

Andy said he was tired. But not too tired to get back

on his bike and ride back to the bike shop. He wobbled and weaved, but his jaw was clenched with determination. Claire didn't want to say anything, but she wondered when Nate would take them back to the suburbs. Her to her house and Andy to the orphanage. She didn't have to ask. Nate brought it up as soon as Andy fell asleep in the back seat on the way back to his place.

"I'll run up and call the orphanage," Nate said. "Before we head back there I need to know what the situation is."

Her mind was full of what-ifs. What if it's still quarantined? What if he has no place to go? She waited in the car with Andy, twisting her fingers into knots. Nate was back in a few minutes with a shopping bag full of the boy's new clothes and toys and, to her surprise, her overnight bag. For a man brought up by strangers, with no permanent woman in his life as of now, he was amazingly thoughtful.

"No answer," he said brusquely. "We'll have to go down there."

"What if...?" she began.

"I don't know," he said. "Let's wait and see."

Claire nodded and no one spoke for most of the hour's drive. The orphanage looked more forlorn in the late-afternoon fog that had rolled in over the hills from the ocean. It also looked deserted. No children were playing in the playground. Shades were drawn on the upper floors.

Nate glanced up at the windows to the infirmary, remembering how it felt to lie there while a fever raged, half-delirious, his mind playing tricks on him. Thinking his mother would come. Waiting for her. He had no idea what it was like to have someone to take care of you and you alone. Sister Evangeline did her best, but how hard it must have been for her to take care of so many kids. How hard it was for her now, now that she was older and sick too.

He sat in front of the orphanage for a long moment, his head in his hands.

He felt Claire's eyes on him and knew she must be wondering what in the hell was wrong with him. And what he was going to do. Or did she know? She had an uncanny way of reading his thoughts.

He lifted his head, looked in the rearview mirror at Andy, whose face was flushed with sleep and said, "I can't do it. I can't take him back there."

"Take him to my house." The relief in her voice was palpable. "I'll keep him until you figure out what to do with him. I can take him to school in the morning and he can come to the library after school. Surely Sister Evangeline would approve. In any case we don't have much choice."

She said "we" but he knew it was his decision. What else could he do but agree? She was willing and he had to get back to town and back to work.

"All right," he said. "I appreciate your taking him in."

Nate felt guilty about taking advantage of Claire. He was sure she didn't see it that way. It was clear she adored the boy and was more than happy to take him. But for how long? What happened next? He carried their things into her house, but when he reached into the back seat to wake Andy, the boy moaned and coughed pitifully.

Nate felt a knot of fear in his chest. "Know anything about how to treat the flu?" he asked Claire who was standing next to the car, her forehead creased with worry lines.

"Just the basics," she said. "Bring him in. I'll look it up on one of the databases I have on my computer."

When Andy woke up, he complained that his head hurt. Before Claire could even turn on her computer she took his temperature. Nate grabbed it out of her hand and when he saw how high it was, he called the doctor on Claire's phone in the kitchen. When he hung up he came back into the living room where she was holding a cool cloth on Andy's forehead.

"Keep him quiet. Under observation. It could be the flu or it could just be a cold. But we can't take a chance," Nate said.

"He said he'd had all his shots," Claire reminded him.

"Yeah, that's right. But when you're a kid, that's what you say, so they don't give you any more."

"Don't worry. Whatever he has, I'll take care of him. He'll be fine," she said, smoothing the hair back from Andy's face.

"What do you mean don't worry?" he said. "How do you know he'll be fine?" He paced back and forth across her living-room carpet, running his hand through his hair until it stood on end. "If you ask me, he's got it. Headaches, high temperature, sneezing, coughing. And most important of all—he's been exposed. That we do know."

"I'll stay home with him," she said. "I have tons of sick leave I've never used. I'll call you if he gets worse."

"Sick leave doesn't cover staying home with a kid who isn't yours, does it? Besides, aren't you in charge? Who opens the library if you're not there?"

"I could make some calls..."

"Isn't it a little late to make calls? Think of all the disappointed patrons if the library doesn't open tomorrow. You're going to work. He's my responsibility. I'm staying here with him."

"Here?" Her eyes widened with shock and surprise.

"I'm sorry if it inconveniences you, but that's the way it's going to be."

"It doesn't inconvenience me," she said. "I thought you had a big meeting tomorrow."

He stopped pacing. "That's right. I completely forgot about it. Unless Andy makes a miraculous recovery, they can have it without me."

She stared at him as if he'd lost his mind. What had he done to make her think he'd abandon the boy now? He had a debt to pay to Sister Evangeline and he was doing it by taking care of her favorite boy. He was sure Sister would expect no less from him.

After a restless night which saw Nate staying in the guest room with Andy, and Claire sleeping in her own room, and all three being awakened by the child's moaning. Claire tiptoed into the bedroom at dawn to find Nate asleep in the rocking chair in the corner, his head resting on his shoulder, his legs stretched out in front of him. There were lines of fatigue at the corners of his eyes, his jaw was shadowed with the beginnings of a beard. Her heart felt like it would burst. To think a man would do this for a child who wasn't his. It was something her father would never have done for her. Of course, she'd never been that sick. If she had been, who would have stepped in?

Quietly, she held the fever strip across Andy's forehead. He was running a high temperature, and he seemed to ache all over. She carried him downstairs to the couch and tempted him with oatmeal and freshly squeezed juice. Then she contemplated calling in sick. Despite what Nate said, she couldn't bear to wake him.

Just as she picked up the phone, Nate came down the stairs, barefoot, wrinkled and blinking owlishly. She thought he'd never looked so appealing. She must have it bad because the man was a mess. Nevertheless she wanted to bury her face in his chest. To wrap her arms around him and spend the day with him and the boy. But of course he wouldn't let her. Nate insisted she go to work.

Stiff and sore from having spent the majority of the night on the floor next to Andy's bed or in the chair in the corner; tired from waking up every hour to put a cold cloth to his forehead, Nate watched Claire ride her bicycle slowly down the street toward the library, craning her neck to look back at him as he stood there.

He couldn't help but think it must make a strange picture of family life. To anyone who didn't know what was going on they'd have wondered why the woman was going off to work while the man stood in the doorway and waved to her. He realized most men wouldn't stay home with a sick kid. But this was not any sick kid. This was an orphan. This was Andy.

Nate turned on the TV in the living room so Andy could watch *Sesame Street* while he made a call to his office.

"You're where?" his partner asked.

"You heard me, I'm in the suburbs taking care of a sick kid."

"Have you lost your mind? We have a meeting in an hour. I'll send Angela there to baby-sit. You've got more important things to do."

"The kid is sick. He's got the flu. He doesn't need a baby-sitter. He needs me. He doesn't need Angela. He doesn't know her. I have to be here."

"What about what's-her-name, the librarian. Why can't she...?"

"She went to work. She can't just stay home unless she's sick. I can. Nobody can fire me. What's the point of owning your own business if you can't take off when you want to?"

"But the contract...!" Paul said.

"I know. I know. But think about it, do we really need more work? Isn't that the reason your marriage is on the rocks, you've been working too hard?"

"Yeah, but..."

"Then let it go."

"Are you okay, Nate? You don't sound like yourself."

"I don't feel like myself much either. You wouldn't either if you'd slept in a chair. I gotta go now. Have Angela call me. I need her to go to my place, bring me some clothes and do some shopping for me."

"Bring you some clothes? How long are you going to be there?"

"I don't know." What he did know was that he wasn't leaving until Andy was well.

He was busy all day. So busy he wondered how even a stay-at-home parent did it. He called the orphanage and left a message about Andy, telling the nun who answered to assure Sister Evangeline that the boy was in good hands. He was glad to hear the sister was up and about but very busy tending to her flock.

He called the doctor and got his advice—bed rest, force fluids. His assistant Angela came by with supplies. He talked to Paul again after the meeting. Claire called and he assured her everything was fine. Andy was napping. No, he hadn't eaten anything. Yes, he was drinking his juice. No, she didn't need to come home. He had everything under control. But did he? He had an uneasy feeling there was something he should be doing but wasn't.

When Claire came in the door at a few minutes after five that evening, he breathed a sigh of relief. Someone to share his worries, his concerns. Someone else to look at Andy and tell him he was doing everything he could. Not that she was a nurse. He didn't need a nurse. He needed a sensible, levelheaded adult who cared about the boy. He needed Claire.

"Lord, I'm glad to see you," he said. He didn't want to admit that he'd been counting the hours since noon.

"What's wrong?" she asked, drawing her eyebrows together.

"Nothing. He fell asleep so I carried him upstairs to the guest room. There's not much change. The doctor said there wouldn't be. Not yet. I'm just glad to see you. It's been a long day."

"I told you I should stay here."

"No way," he said flatly. "I'm not leaving until he gets well. I know I'm in the way, but it can't be helped."

"You're not in the way," she said. But she knew he didn't believe her. They went upstairs to look at Andy.

His face was flushed and he was tossing and turning restlessly.

"Poor kid," she whispered, kneeling on the floor and pressing her palm against his forehead. "It doesn't seem possible. Yesterday he was bursting with energy, making pancakes, eating, riding in the park. Now look at him.'' She stood and blinked back a tear. "How ironic, his fortune said he'd have health and happiness.''

He took her hand and held it tightly. "He'll get his health back. And yesterday he had a large dose of happiness. Yesterday was a special day. For him and for me,'' he said.

Her lower lip trembled. "Me too,'' she said softly.

"When he gets well we'll do it again.''

"Are you sure he's going to get well?''

"Absolutely. It may take a week or two, but we'll see him back to normal.'' He didn't mention the danger of pneumonia. The doctor had told him it was a possible complication, but assured him it wasn't likely, so why worry Claire any more than she already was?

"I wish we could do something more for him,'' she said.

"We're doing everything we can,'' he said. "Rest and fluids every few hours.''

"You've been doing this all day. No wonder you look tired.'' Her gaze scanned his face. She reached over and smoothed the worry lines in his forehead he didn't even know he had. Her touch was so gentle and soothing he felt a tight knot of worry in his chest start to dissolve. It was a strange feeling. He was used to bottling up any tension he felt. He had long ago learned to keep his feelings to himself. Now he wanted to share them. He realized he'd been so intent on glossing over Andy's sickness and his own concern, and taking care of business by phone, that he'd been dealing with his worries in his usual way. Until she walked in the door.

"I'm fine," he said. "But I could use some food. How does roast chicken and creamed spinach sound?"

"Don't tell me you…?"

"I didn't make it, I'm strictly a pancakes guy, but I did have the sense to order it."

He was rewarded for his thoughtfulness with her grateful smile. For that smile he might even be tempted to learn to cook.

Over the dinner he'd had Angela pick up in town and bring along with a suitcase full of his clothes from his house, he told Claire everything he'd learned about the flu, what was happening at the orphanage and even what he'd learned from his partner about the meeting at his office. As he talked and ate, he forgot his fatigue. He felt like an overflowing vessel, spilling his guts once again to the librarian who had turned listening into an art.

It was strange for a loner like himself to talk so much over dinner. But he realized that along with food, he needed company. He needed the company of someone who shared his concerns. Who was naturally sympathetic. Who looked at him with eyes filled with understanding and sympathy. Usually he stopped on the way home from his office at his favorite restaurant and ate a solitary dinner. Usually he felt no need to talk to anyone at the end of the day. Usually he was talked out, kept his big problems to himself. But these were not usual times. And Claire was a great sounding board, making perceptive comments and asking pertinent questions.

"You're a good listener," he said, "you know that?"

"You are too," she said, as she cleared the plates

and put them in the sink. "This is the third night we've spent talking."

"You mean *I've* spent talking," he said. "You haven't told me about your day."

Over coffee in the living room where she sat on one end of the couch with her legs tucked under her and he sat at the other, she told him about the problems getting the bookmobile, complaints about fines, "dirty" books and the absent high-school girl who usually came in after school to shelve books.

"But I couldn't concentrate," she admitted. "I kept thinking about Andy and you and wishing I was home with you," she said wistfully. "If I had a sick child I'd stay home with him…or her. I'd quit my job before I'd leave them alone."

"What if your husband stayed home?" he asked.

"What husband?" Claire asked lightly. She set her cup on the coffee table and turned to him. "It's easier to imagine having a child than being married." She was lying. She could imagine. All day long she'd imagined what it would be like to be married. It wasn't hard at all. She'd imagined that she had the kind of husband who'd stay home with a sick child. Who was strong and tough and kind and sensitive. Who resembled the man at the end of her couch. Who had no idea what a great father he'd make. Who thought you had to have come from a happy, two-parent home to know how to make your own two-parent home. That's what she used to think. Until now. Until this weekend when she started to believe, to hope, to dream.

He frowned. "I thought…do you *want* to get married?" he asked. "Because if you do…"

"Yes?" Her heart stopped beating. The silence in the room stretched for long minutes. Her gaze was locked with his. Her mouth was so dry she couldn't speak if she'd wanted to.

Finally he broke the spell. "If you do, then say so. Go for it. You'd make a great wife. But what was all that about a career being enough? I thought we both agreed that a career was enough." He surveyed her closely, letting his gaze travel over her body. "I'd marry you myself if I was getting married. You're a good cook, you're a good listener. You've got a great body under all those clothes...." He reached over and casually unbuttoned the top button on her shirt and traced her collarbone with his fingers. His expression turned serious. His concentration zeroed in on her. The touch of his hand sent a shiver down her spine and heat spiraling to the core of her being.

"Don't," she said in a tight voice.

"Don't what?" he asked, leaning toward her to bridge the gap between them, threading his hand through her hair and brushing her lips with his. "Don't tell you how sexy you are? Don't tell you how hard it is to keep my hands off you? How irresistible you are? How much I want to take those ridiculous clothes off you?"

He pressed her breasts against his chest, so close she could feel his heart pounding through his shirt. What if he took her clothes off and she took his off and there was nothing between them at all? What then? What if they made love? Right there on her couch. The thought of it made her weak with desire.

She'd never felt this way about anyone. She knew she'd never feel this way about anyone else. But making love with Nate wouldn't change anything, she thought sadly. He still wouldn't want to marry her or anyone. And she'd be left with a broken heart and broken dreams and a crumpled fortune from a cookie, that would never come true.

She dragged herself out of his arms and took a deep breath. "I'll go check on Andy," she said.

Chapter Nine

Chapter Nine

That night Claire insisted that Nate take her bed. He looked tired. He'd also looked shocked when she'd jumped up from the couch. What did he think, that she was the type for a quick affair? If so, he didn't know her very well. He didn't protest very long. He must have seen the determination in her eyes. Heard it in her voice. So he gave in. But after he'd said goodnight, told her to call him if she needed him, he gave her a long look she could have sworn was filled with longing or regret or both. Then he disappeared into her bedroom.

She stood in the hall staring at the door he shut behind him. Her knees wobbled. Her heart pounded. She knew what she wanted from him, but what did he want from her?

It was her turn to sleep in the rocking chair next to Andy's bed. It wasn't comfortable, but she was afraid to leave the boy, afraid he'd wake up and call her. In the morning she was stiff and exhausted. Nate looked better. She told him so.

"Must be your bed," he said running his hand through his unruly hair. "Your sheets. They smell like you. Like spring flowers. Almost as good as sleeping with you." He gave her a slow smile. "But not quite."

She didn't answer. What did he expect her to say? She said goodbye to Andy and rode her bike down the street with Nate's words in her ear, the image of his face in front of her as she wove in and out of traffic, ignoring honking horns and stop signs.

All week it was more of the same. Sometimes he teased her and flirted with her. Other times he talked to her seriously and listened to her just as seriously. He complimented her and fed her with take-out food. She appreciated his efforts, but tried not to take them seriously. She couldn't afford a broken heart. Andy slowly got well. And she knew it was just a matter of time before she lost them both: Andy to a foster home and Nate to his real life.

Andy was well enough that she and Nate felt okay about sleeping on the couch or in her bedroom. Not together of course. Whenever Nate got close or said something suggestive, she moved away or changed the subject. He'd clench his jaw, but look unrepentant and try again the next time. She was already suffering from separation anxiety and neither one of them had even left. The next weekend they talked about the future. Nate explained to Andy he was going back to the orphanage as soon as he was well, until they found him a suitable foster home with two parents. His eyes filled with tears.

"But I thought you and Claire…?" he said.

"Claire and I are not a foster family," Nate explained. "We're not any kind of family. But she'll still be at the library. You can go to story hour after school just the way you always did. But you can't run away again. Is that clear?" he said. "Sister Evangeline was worried about you. She cares about you."

Andy didn't speak. He pressed his lips together and Claire was worried. Worried they'd never find him a family. Worried he'd run away again. The day he was finally well enough to go back and the orphanage had lifted the quarantine was the worst day of her life. She couldn't go with Nate to take him back. She just couldn't stand to see him disappear behind the brick walls. It was hard enough to see him leave her house.

She packed his belongings, the toys and the clothes Nate had bought him, and hugged him tightly, biting her lip to keep from crying. He went back upstairs for a toy he'd forgotten and Nate caught her by the elbow. "Look," he said. "This isn't easy for me either."

"Then don't take him."

"What should I do with him?"

"Leave him here," she said.

"We've been through that," he said. "You don't qualify as a foster family. You're not married and you have a full-time job. But you can see him whenever you want to. I've arranged that with Sister. Take him for an occasional weekend if you'd like. That's what I plan to do. Until they find a family for him."

I want to be his family, she thought. "What about you? I supposed you're not qualified either," she said. She knew the answer to that. He'd put in his time. He'd taken care of Andy when he was sick, as no one else could or would have done. Now he was going back to work. He must be relieved it was over. Nate had never complained but it must have felt like being in prison for two weeks.

"Me? I'm not cut out for fatherhood," he said curtly. "You know that."

"Then go. Just get it over with," she said.

He nodded and called Andy. Before Claire could hug him again, Nate hustled the boy out of the house and into his car.

That was when she lost it completely. She couldn't even watch them get into the car. Blindly she made her way out the back door into the yard, sat on the wooden bench in the middle of the overgrown grass and sobbed. She felt as hollow as if her insides had been ripped out.

She knew she shouldn't have fallen in love with Nate or Andy, but she had. She was only human. Before they had come into her life she'd been content to be a children's librarian. She'd had children in her life, but they were always someone else's children. Now she wanted her own children. She wanted Andy, and she wanted a husband too. She wanted Nate. She knew she couldn't have him, but that didn't stop her from crying until she was drained of all emotion. She staggered into the house, fell into her bed and slept for twelve hours.

When she woke up she washed her face, combed her hair and looked in the mirror. She looked like hell. But she didn't have to look like hell. Nate had told her she was sexy, and he'd made her feel beautiful. The next day after work she went shopping. She bought sweaters and skirts and slacks and they all fit her, showing off her body in a way she wouldn't have dreamed of before she'd met Nate.

She stood in front of the three-way mirror in the

dressing room and realized she was a different person now. Sadder and wiser, but proud too. Proud of the way she looked. Proud of the way she felt. Like a woman with a past that was best forgotten and a future to look forward to. A future without Nate, to be sure, but still a future.

"Stunning," the saleswoman murmured. "What I wouldn't give for your figure. I always say, if you've got it, flaunt it."

"That's what I've been told," Claire murmured. "Wrap it up. I'll take it all."

She arranged to pick up Andy the next Saturday and take him out for the day. While waiting for Andy, she met Sister Evangeline for the first time and was surprised to find how tiny and frail she was. She didn't look like someone who wielded so much power, until Claire felt the strong grip of her fingers when the older woman shook her hand.

"I've heard so much about you," Sister Evangeline said, motioning Claire to sit down in a chair across from her desk.

Claire smiled. She was about to say the same about the diminutive nun. "I hope Andy said good things about me," she said.

"He did, and so did Nate," Sister said.

Claire blushed furiously. She felt the nun's eyes on her, assessing her reaction. She wondered what exactly Nate had said.

"Nate tells me you're a librarian and that you're fond of children," Sister Evangeline said. "He didn't say how very attractive you are."

No, she thought. He wouldn't. But did he say I'm fond of him? she wanted to ask. *Did he tell you I've fallen in love with him? Or does he even know or care?*

"I'm especially fond of Andy," Claire said, hoping to get off the subject of Nate. "Even before he got sick and stayed at my house, he was one of my favorite children."

"And now?" the nun prompted.

"I confess I've fallen in love with the boy." She hadn't intended to tell her this, but the nun's wise blue gaze inspired confidence. "I'd adopt him in a minute, if I could. But as you may know, I have a full-time job and I'm not married. I know enough about children to know that if possible, it's best for them to have a two-parent family. I myself was raised by my father and...and..." She couldn't continue without going into the story of her life and she knew the nun didn't have time or interest in hearing it.

"What about Nate?" the nun asked.

Claire didn't know what to say. She didn't know what the nun was getting at. Did she mean, have you fallen in love with him too? Or, would he adopt Andy? Or what?

When Claire didn't answer, the sister continued. "Nate is a wonderfully kind and caring man. You may not know that because he keeps his feelings hidden from the world. Understandable considering his background. I'm just grateful we had the opportunity to play a part in his upbringing. But there is just so much we could do for him. He's very successful, but I wish he had as much love in his life as he has money. The love of an octogenarian nun just isn't enough. Not for a man like Nate. He needs someone to share his life with. Someone he can trust. Someone who won't abandon him when the chips are down."

Don't we all, Claire thought. "He speaks very highly of you too," she said.

Sister Evangeline smiled. "And of you. Now I see why. I have a confession for you. Before we met, I wondered if you were good enough for him."

"For Nate?" Claire asked, pressing her hands together. "Oh, but I'm not the person he's looking for….I mean, of course he can trust me and I certainly would never abandon him, but unfortunately, he's not…"

"Oh, but he is," the nun said. "He's in love with you."

Claire stared at the tiny figure behind the large desk in amazement. Sister Evangeline might be insightful, wise and wonderful, but she was dead wrong about this. She'd obviously decided that it would solve all of Andy's problems if Nate and Claire would jointly take custody of Andy. And how best to do that? By falling in love and getting married to each other.

"That's a lovely thought," Claire said sadly. "But I'm afraid it isn't quite accurate to say he's in love with me, no matter how convenient that would be for Andy. I don't know what Nate said to you, but his feelings for me, if any, are more likely respect and admiration, at least I hope they are." She was proud of herself for sounding so mature and levelheaded when inside her heart was breaking.

"That sounds like the basis of a happy marriage," Sister Evangeline said serenely.

"Yes, but…"

"But you're not in love with him, is that the problem?" she asked.

Those bright blue eyes bored right through Claire. She knew it was useless to lie. The nun would know the truth. So she didn't. She'd already said far too much. She changed the subject.

"Have you had any luck finding a family for Andy?" she asked.

"I believe I have," the nun said with a quiet smile. "I believe I have."

Disturbed by the calm serenity in the sister's voice, Claire excused herself and left the office lost in thought. She couldn't shake the feeling that the nun knew more than she did about some things, yes. About other things, like Nate's feelings for her, a definite no.

Claire spent a fun-filled day with Andy. She'd bought a secondhand bike for him and they rode to a nearby park together. They'd been in close touch: she'd seen him after school during story hour at the library so she didn't have to pepper him with questions about his school or his life back at the orphanage. If a new foster family was in the offing as Sister Evangeline had hinted, Andy appeared to know nothing about it. Perhaps, in view of his last escape from the orphanage, the nuns felt it was best to keep any plans for him a secret until finalized.

"You look different, Ms. Claire," Andy said, tilting his head to one side to observe her as he munched on his sandwich at the picnic table.

"Just plain Claire, Andy. Thank you." She accepted it as a compliment. It wasn't the first she'd received since she'd changed her looks. But better than looking different on the outside, she felt different on the inside. She felt like a desirable woman. She knew that Nate had desired her. He'd made that plain. But it had taken a while to sink in. She wasn't beautiful, she knew that. That wasn't important. What was important was that she was proud of how she looked, that she was no longer ashamed of her body, no longer tried to cover it up. She didn't think she was actually flaunting it, as the saleswoman had suggested, but she wasn't hiding it either.

It had taken several trips, but she'd replaced most of her wardrobe with the help of a kind personal shopper at the department store. Instead of wearing her hair tucked behind her ears, she'd had it shaped and now let it in swing free against her cheeks. Her clothes were still shirts and sweaters and pants and skirts, just as she'd always worn, but now they fit. They clung to her body the way clothes are supposed to.

"What'll we do tomorrow?" Claire asked the boy when they arrived back at her house. She'd cleared it with Sister Evangeline that she'd have him overnight.

"Nate's coming to get me at nine o'clock," he said.

Claire's heart lurched. "Does he know you're here?" she asked.

"Yep. Sister told him."

"But I thought…" This was awkward. They hadn't planned this very well, she and Nate. She'd thought they'd alternate weekends with Andy. But he must think they were alternating days. She'd have to give him a call. She didn't want to give him a call. She didn't want to leave a message on his machine the way the other women did. Begging, pleading him to call back. Trying to make him feel guilty.

So she got out the Scrabble game and tried to think about something else. When he came tomorrow she'd be cool and polite. She'd graciously allow Andy to go off with Nate even though she had tickets for that ice show with his favorite cartoon characters that Andy had once asked to see. She wouldn't even mention it.

* * *

On his way to get Andy, Nate stopped by the orphanage to have a few words with Sister Evangeline. He wished he could pick up Andy there so he wouldn't have to see Claire again. He knew she thought he was heartless, taking Andy back to the orphanage, insisting that a foster family be found for him when she wanted to take him in herself. Hell, he would have taken him too, but it wasn't in the kid's best interest. She of all people should know that. She knew what it was like to be raised by a single parent. And he knew there had to be decent people out there who'd appreciate the boy. In the meantime Sister had sent for him again and once again he couldn't say no to her.

"Are you feeling better?" he asked when she'd invited him into her office, the same office where he'd been summoned so often as a child.

"Very well, thank you," she said. "I had the opportunity to meet your librarian yesterday."

He stifled a smile at her choice of words and repressed the urge to deny she was *his* librarian. Obviously the good sister was up to something. It did no good to try to second-guess her. He only hoped he'd be half as sharp at her age.

"She seems perfectly qualified to be a mother to Andy."

Nate's mouth fell open in surprise. "What? I thought it was always preferable…"

"For a child to have a two-parent family. Of course it is. Therefore we must find Ms. Cooper a husband."

"Sister, aren't you busy enough without running a matchmaking bureau?" he teased while his brain was in turmoil. Find Claire a husband? How would they do that?

Sister Evangeline wasn't amused. She was deadly

serious. And equally determined. "I'm never too busy to look after my flock. I have many children to take care of, but as of this moment, Andy is my number-one priority. I know what you've done for the boy. I know that you've sacrificed your time and energy, but I'm asking you to go one step further. I'm asking you to marry Claire Cooper."

The room spun around. His first thought was that now he knew how Claire felt the day she'd fainted. His mouth was dry, and his head felt like it was floating above his body. Had she really said what he thought she'd said?

"Don't tell me it hasn't occurred to you," Sister Evangeline said. "She's a lovely woman. What are you looking for, Nathaniel?" she asked sternly.

"Looking for? I'm not looking, Sister. I'm perfectly happy on my own. I don't need anyone else in my life. Especially not a wife." He should have known better. She could always tell when he was lying. Her blue eyes pierced the protective shell that no one else had ever penetrated and saw right into his soul.

He laid his hands out, palms flat on her desk and exhaled loudly. "All right, it has occurred to me. I grew attached to Claire during the weeks I spent at her house. I find her attractive and intelligent and, as you say, perfectly qualified to be a mother to Andy." And to other children as well. A whole passel of bright, spunky children with big brown eyes and long lashes and a tendency to blush when embarrassed. He was looking at Sister Evangeline, but he was seeing these imaginary children sitting around a table playing board games in front of a roaring fire, or biking single-file down a country road. Sister's mouth was moving.

She was talking to him, but he didn't hear a word she said.

When the images finally faded, he got up, thanked Sister, and walked out of the orphanage. She stood in the doorway, and he felt her eyes on him as he went to his car. He had no idea what he'd agreed to or how they'd left the issue of Claire and Andy and himself. He only knew he was a changed man. How and when he'd changed, he wasn't sure. But it had started here at the orphanage a few weeks ago and he somehow felt it was going to end here too. He rolled his window down and waved to the nun in the doorway. She waved back. And smiled confidently.

Claire came to the front door. He stood staring at her as if he'd never seen her before. It had only been a week, but what a week! Somehow she'd undergone a transformation. A subtle one, but as a detective he was trained to notice subtle changes. She was wearing a ribbed T-shirt and slim stretch jeans. She had the most glorious body he'd ever seen. Yes, he'd seen it before, but he was seeing it in a new light. She held herself with new confidence, as if she was as aware of her femininity as he was. He knew one thing. If he didn't marry her, someone else would. *Over his dead body*.

He too had had an eventful week. He'd rearranged his schedule, given most of his cases to the young, eager novices and relieved both himself and Paul of much of the workload. He'd ordered Paul to take a few weeks off to see if a break would change his outlook as much as it had his. He didn't think his change of attitude had anything to do with Claire, but now he knew it had. It had everything to do with her and with Andy.

"Come in," she said. "He's almost ready."

"What about you?" he asked, his eyes never leaving her face.

"I had him yesterday. This is your day," she said.

"I've got tickets for the circus," he said. "Three tickets. I thought we'd all go."

"I didn't know the circus was in town. I've never been to one," she said.

"I know. Your father thought it was childish."

"We can't go through life making up for what we missed as children," she said.

"How *will* we go through life then?" he asked. He really didn't know. If she wouldn't go through life with him, he didn't know what he'd do. There was a long pause. He took a deep breath. "How about together?" he suggested. He waited. And waited. She couldn't say no, could she? "I love you, Claire."

It took a while for his words to register. Then she threw herself into his arms and pressed her face against his chest. She was laughing and crying at the same time.

"I love you too," she said. "But do you really mean you want to…go through life all together—forever?" she asked.

"I mean it," he said, his whole body flooded with relief. He hadn't known what she'd say. Hell, he hadn't known what *he'd* say until he walked into the house, but he knew how it had to be. How it was meant to be. Him and Claire and Andy. Together. Forever.

Epilogue

They didn't hold many weddings in the chapel of the Sacred Heart Children's Home, but this was a special occasion. The groom had grown up there, and the boy who brought them together had also called it his home until recently. The nuns wore their white robes. Sister Evangeline played a prelude of sacred music on the organ while the guests took their seats. The choir sang a Bach chorale they'd been practising for weeks that filled the church with joyful music.

The little chapel was full of children from the orphanage, and children who were patrons of story hour at the library who'd come to see Ms. Cooper get married to a real live detective. Just like in a book.

As the ring bearer, and as the boy who'd brought the bride and groom together, Andy took his responsibilities seriously. He was dressed appropriately in his very first suit, tie and vest, as he waited at the altar with the ring in his pocket.

The bride wore a long traditional gown of white

satin with long sleeves and a fitted bodice that made her look like a goddess. At least that's what the groom thought as he waited at the altar. His eyes never left her radiant face. His expression was solemn. After waiting his whole life for her, he was still impatient to hear the words that would bind her to him forever.

"I now pronounce you man and wife."

Nate hadn't smiled during the entire ceremony until now. With Claire's arm in his, they walked down the aisle together, beaming at each other. The happy faces on either side of the aisle were a blur. The wedding was over, but his life was just beginning. His and Claire's and Andy's. Their life together.

His recurrent dream of the happy family around the dinner table was finally going to come true. He and Claire had decided to give Andy as many brothers and sisters as would fit around that table. Which would mean slowing down their once-all-consuming, challenging careers. At least for a while.

The music swelled and the only person happier than Claire and Nate and Andy was Sister Evangeline who took special pride in that moment. She was too humble to take credit for bringing the two of them together, but she said a small prayer that everyone's secret wish would come true—as hers had—that all her children would go out in the world and find a love as beautiful as Nate and Claire's.

* * * * *

Silhouette Romance
proudly presents a brand-new, four-book heartwarming series...

STORKVILLE USA

Welcome to Storkville, USA, where matchmaking twin babies make love happen for four unsuspecting couples!

On sale August 2000:
THOSE MATCHMAKING BABIES
by **Marie Ferrarella** (SR #1462)

On sale September 2000:
HIS EXPECTANT NEIGHBOR
by **Susan Meier** (SR #1468)

On sale October 2000:
THE ACQUIRED BRIDE
by **Teresa Southwick** (SR #1474)

On sale November 2000:
HER HONOR-BOUND LAWMAN
by **Karen Rose Smith** (SR #1480)

Only from

▼ *Silhouette* ROMANCE™

Available at your favorite retail outlet.

Visit Silhouette at www.eHarlequin.com   SRSVUSA

If you enjoyed what you just read,
then we've got an offer you can't resist!

Take 2 bestselling love stories FREE!
Plus get a FREE surprise gift!

Clip this page and mail it to Silhouette Reader Service™

IN U.S.A.	IN CANADA
3010 Walden Ave.	P.O. Box 609
P.O. Box 1867	Fort Erie, Ontario
Buffalo, N.Y. 14240-1867	L2A 5X3

YES! Please send me 2 free Silhouette Romance® novels and my free surprise gift. Then send me 6 brand-new novels every month, which I will receive months before they're available in stores. In the U.S.A., bill me at the bargain price of $2.90 plus 25¢ delivery per book and applicable sales tax, if any*. In Canada, bill me at the bargain price of $3.25 plus 25¢ delivery per book and applicable taxes**. That's the complete price and a savings of at least 10% off the cover prices—what a great deal! I understand that accepting the 2 free books and gift places me under no obligation ever to buy any books. I can always return a shipment and cancel at any time. Even if I never buy another book from Silhouette, the 2 free books and gift are mine to keep forever. So why not take us up on our invitation. You'll be glad you did!

215 SEN C24Q
315 SEN C24R

Name	(PLEASE PRINT)	
Address	Apt.#	
City	State/Prov.	Zip/Postal Code

* Terms and prices subject to change without notice. Sales tax applicable in N.Y.
** Canadian residents will be charged applicable provincial taxes and GST.
All orders subject to approval. Offer limited to one per household.
® are registered trademarks of Harlequin Enterprises Limited.

SROM00_R   ©1998 Harlequin Enterprises Limited

Silhouette

where love comes alive—online...

your romantic
life

➤ Talk to Dr. Romance, find a romantic recipe, or send a virtual hint to the love of your life. You'll find great articles and advice on romantic issues that are close to your heart.

your romantic
books

➤ Visit our *Author's Alcove* and try your hand in the Writing Round Robin—contribute a chapter to an online book in the making.

➤ Enter the *Reading Room* for an interactive novel—help determine the fate of a story being created now by one of your favorite authors.

➤ Drop into *Shop eHarlequin* to buy the latest releases— read an excerpt, write a review and find this month's Silhouette top sellers.

your romantic
escapes

➤ Escape into romantic movies at *Reel Love*, learn what the stars have in store for you with *Lovescopes*, treat yourself to our *Indulgences Guides* and get away to the latest romantic hot spots in *Romantic Travel*.

All this and more available at
www.eHarlequin.com
on Women.com Networks

SECHAN1R

Desire celebrates Silhouette's 20th anniversary in grand style!

Don't miss:

• *The Dakota Man* by Joan Hohl
Another unforgettable MAN OF THE MONTH
On sale October 2000

• *Marriage Prey* by Annette Broadrick
Her special anniversary title!
On sale November 2000

• *Slow Fever* by Cait London
Part of her new miniseries FREEDOM VALLEY
On sale December 2000

Plus:

FORTUNE'S CHILDREN: THE GROOMS
On sale August through December 2000
Exciting new titles from Leanne Banks, Kathryn Jensen,
Shawna Delacorte, Caroline Cross and Peggy Moreland

Every woman wants to be loved...
BODY & SOUL
Desire's highly sensuous new promotion features stories
from Jennifer Greene, Anne Marie Winston
and Dixie Browning!

Available at your favorite retail outlet.

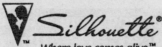

Where love comes alive™

Visit Silhouette at www.eHarlequin.com

PS20SD

**Don't miss
an exciting opportunity
to save on the purchase of
Harlequin and Silhouette books!**

Buy any two Harlequin or
Silhouette books and save
$10.00 off future Harlequin
and Silhouette purchases

OR

buy any three
Harlequin or Silhouette books
and save **$20.00 off** future
Harlequin and Silhouette purchases.

**Watch for details
coming in October 2000!**

PHQ400

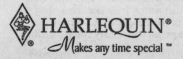

Silhouette
ROMANCE™

COMING NEXT MONTH

#1474 THE ACQUIRED BRIDE—Teresa Southwick
Storkville, USA
Single mother Dana Hewitt would do anything to keep her kids—even agree to a convenient marriage with tycoon Quentin McCormack! But then she began dreaming of being his real bride—in every sense of the word....

#1475 JESSIE'S EXPECTING—Kasey Michaels
The Chandlers Request...
Sweet Jessie Chandler had always loved Matthew Garvey from afar. But he had never noticed her—until an innocent kiss led to an unexpected night of passion. What would Matthew's reaction be once he learned Jessie's expecting?

#1476 SNOWBOUND SWEETHEART—Judy Christenberry
The Circle K Sisters
When city gal Lindsay Crawford became snowbound with handsome rancher Gil Daniels, she couldn't help falling for him. But he thought she wouldn't be happy with country living forever. Could she convince him that her home was where *he* was?

#1477 THE NANNY PROPOSAL—Donna Clayton
Single Doctor Dads
Greg Hamilton had his hands full raising his ten-month-old baby, and Jane Dale's motherly touch was just what the doctor ordered. Although Greg wasn't looking for a wife, seeing his pretty nanny rocking his baby triggered some unsettling feelings in his bachelor heart....

#1478 RAISING BABY JANE—Lilian Darcy
Allie Todd had vowed never to get close to another man again. Yet sharing close quarters with Connor Callahan while caring for her six-month-old niece had forged a bond between them that couldn't be denied—just like the secret she was keeping about the maternity of baby Jane....

#1479 ONE FIANCÉE TO GO, PLEASE—Jackie Braun
To secure the job of his dreams, Jack Maris asked Tess Donovan to pose as his fiancée. Savoring the distraction from her demanding life, Tess agreed. But when word of their engagement spread, they kept up the charade. And then things got deliciously complicated....

CMN0900